Three Valleys Ranch

Three Valleys Ranch

To Mary,

Merry Christmas & Happy Holidays. I hope you enjoy the book.

Kenny W. Duncan

12-23-06

Kenny W. Duncan

Copyright © 2007 by Kenny W. Duncan.

ISBN 10 :	Hardcover	1-4257-3740-4
	Softcover	1-4257-3739-0
ISBN 13 :	Hardcover	978-1-425737-40-5
	Softcover	978-1-425737-39-9

All rights reserved. No part of this book may be reproduced or transmitted in any form or by any means, electronic or mechanical, including photocopying, recording, or by any information storage and retrieval system, without permission in writing from the copyright owner.

This is a work of fiction. Names, characters, places and incidents either are the product of the author's imagination or are used fictitiously, and any resemblance to any actual persons, living or dead, events, or locales is entirely coincidental.

This book was printed in the United States of America.

To order additional copies of this book, contact:
Xlibris Corporation
1-888-795-4274
www.Xlibris.com
Orders@Xlibris.com

To all the friends and family and strangers who had read the previous book, "The Big Bay" and asked me "When's the next book coming out, I can't wait" . . . Thanks, that was great inspiration . . .

And a big thanks to my family who inherited the job of editing my typing and picture taking . . .

Chapter 1

Wade Tavner was a man driven by a strong will to achieve the goals of his own life. He grew up in the Midwest, in the northern part of Missouri. He had been taught to shoot straight as a young boy by his father, growing up in hard times, whether it was a deer or a squirrel, one shot was all that was required to kill your prey, no waste of powder or lead, or wasting of good meat when the shot was placed with accuracy. Wade had endured the hardships of the War Between the States, losing both parents, and being caught up in the border wars that followed . . .

He had learned to fight at an early age and had spent time riding with Quantrill . . . Shooting and killing became a way of life, and there was none better at riding and shooting from the back of a horse as Wade Tavner . . .

But he had grown tired and weary of that way of life and ventured off into the wilds, west of the big rivers. Into new territories yet to be discovered and tamed . . . Trying to stay clear of trouble and of gunfights that would brand a man as trouble to where ever he would choose to roam, he just wished to be left alone, to live his own life . . . But a man with pride that wouldn't allow himself to turn and walk away from trouble, whether it was an injustice to himself or to another . . . He had walked a fine line between right and wrong, and sometimes felt that what he was told was right, might not have been so black and white . . . Wade had taught himself to trust no man, for good or bad or right or wrong . . . A man has to take a stand on his own sooner or later for what he believes to be the truth . . .

Wade had learned to stay clear of most towns, as they seemed to attract trouble for a drifting man as he . . . He had put more than a man or two in the ground from gunfights . . . He was quick and calculating, and had a cold cruel look in his eyes that showed no fear of death . . . He donned a mustache, which turned in a downward position that never revealed a smile, if he ever did. His face was tanned dark from riding under the sun for years and gave it a leathery look with crevices around the corners of his cold blue steel grey eyes, with a crease across his forehead from squinting against the sun parched ground that he had covered over time, all of which his facial features gave him an even meaner look than what he actually projected . . . He was a man of average height with wide shoulders and a lean waist, strong muscular arms and back that packed a power that was unequaled by men fifty pounds heavier . . . The man carried not an ounce of fat on his body, it was a body tuned for hard work . . . Obstacles were simply that, he was a man determined to finish whatever task he started . . .

Wade had traveled most of the west in the past few years picking up various jobs throughout his roaming and discovering the world at his feet or at the feet of his steed. A man who values a good horse as one of the most valuable things a man could own out here, a man's life could depend on his horse at any given time. Wade had an eye for good horseflesh, something he had learned from his father back in Missouri. Wade could always size up the best horse in the lot with quick and precise judgment. Good confirmation was a must, but the first priority was good solid feet, a horse was only as good as his worst hoof . . . Wade had an eye for horses with black hooves . . . White socks always looked a little flashier, but nothing better than hard black hooves for hard riding and endurance and long wear . . .

Wade Tavner had worked jobs as a ranch hand on ranches from the hill country of Texas to the breaks of the big river in Montana, driving cattle from Texas through the summer months to the high ranges of Montana, where he stayed on to work cattle and learned to love the mountains and the surrounding areas. After the big storms of one of the worst winters in that area which put most ranches out of business, Wade moved farther south and took up a job of driver for McNall Freighting Company. A job that fit Wade well as he traveled even more extensively throughout the western region of this country. A dangerous job that paid him well as he always volunteered for the lone routes that would take him deeper into the country . . . Most freighters traveled in wagons of ten or more, but once to their distribution areas which based itself in Denver, the loads had to be split up and sent out into smaller lots, the individual wagons were the ones more apt to be picked off by ambushers . . . It was hard to get most men to take these routes, but Wade Tavner had confidence in his own abilities that he feared not an ambush . . . . He preferred these trips as it took him to new places he hadn't seen before and he preferred traveling alone. It kept his old senses of the old days of living that way sharp and keen . . . There had been two occasions where there had been an ambush attempt on his wagon of freight, and both times he carried the bodies of the men back into the closest town tied across their own horses . . . Unaware of it, he was building a reputation in the west, something he did not want to follow him around and haunt him through life . . . Although folks here knew nothing of his life of riding and killing in the border wars, there were those who always suspected something, He was just too good with a gun, and an air of confidence of himself that showed itself to others, unknowingly to Wade himself . . .

On this trip north, Wade had backed his boss in an argument that turned bad in Ft. Laramie, where he shot and killed the two men in the street and one on the boardwalk in front of the army corps office, and the one man was already holding a gun on them, word like that traveled fast and grew each time it was told . . . . By the time Wade had ridden back to Denver, a month later the story was well over exaggerated . . . .

Wade had drove through an area several days north and west of Denver that appealed to him above all other places, the grass seemed to be greener and taller than anywhere he had been, and there was plenty of water, enough water to run a good sized herd of cattle and horses, and far from other folks who had come into the area . . . He wanted a quiet place, a place virgin to other folks . . . A place hard to find, off the regular trails that had led over the passes of the area . . . This valley was not wide at any one point, but stretched out for miles running along the river that flowed through it . . . Peaks that reached high into the surrounding mountains, a place protected from the harsh cold winds from the west, Wade had learned that from the winter in Montana.

Wade Tavner realized it was time for him to move on, things had changed here, people looked at him a different way now, there was even an article about the shooting in Laramie in the paper here, and it was highly exaggerated as well . . .

There were two things bothering him now, Wade wanted to go back to the valley he had found a year earlier in his travels and homestead the place to call his own, the wandering days were growing old and weary for him, he longed now to settle down, and Wade had met a woman, a woman who he knew only as Mary, he met her in Ft. Douglas, delivering goods there to a general store and feed mercantile . . .

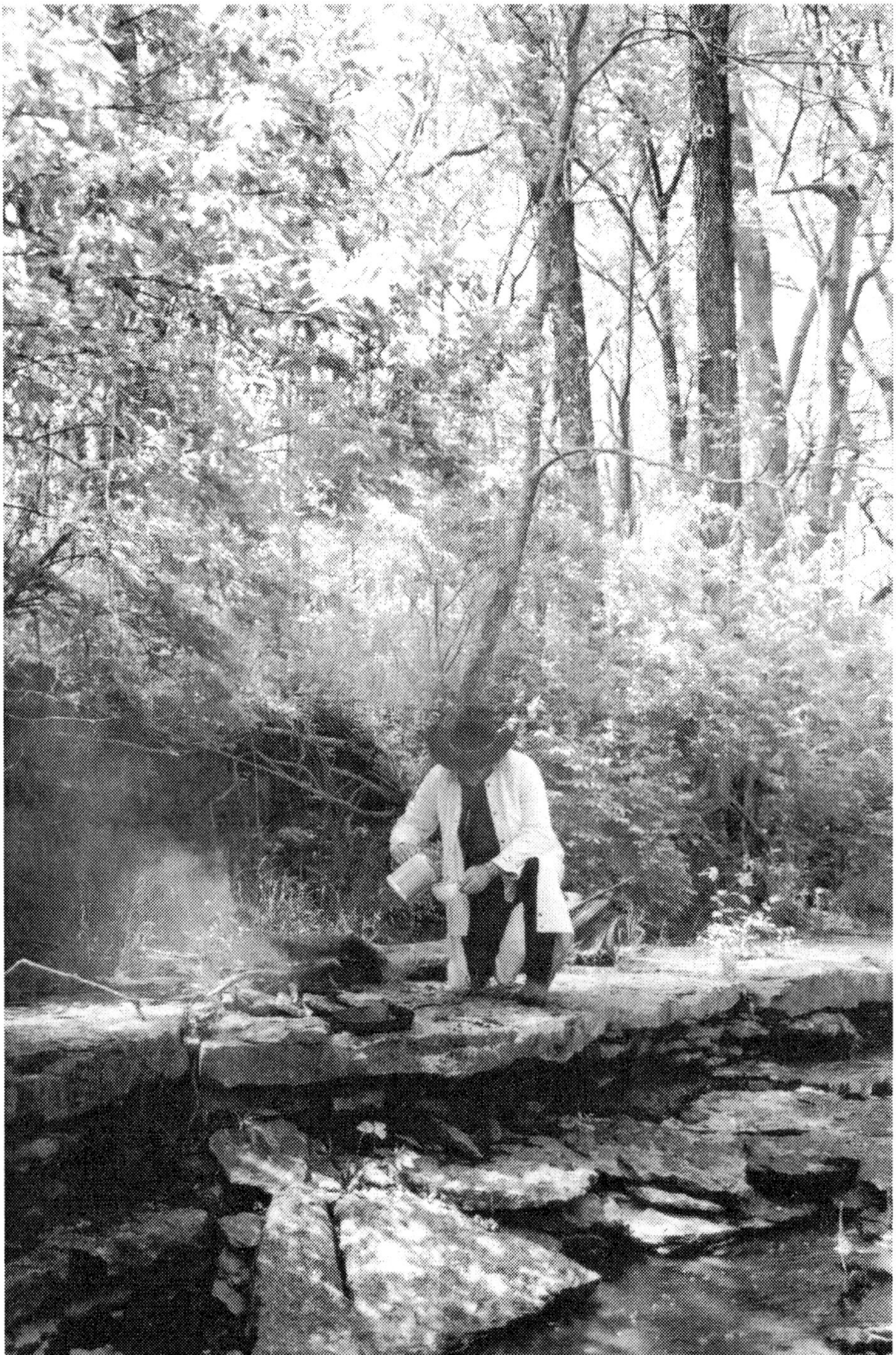

Chapter 2

Mary Franks was filling an order of goods for Mrs. Brown when the freight wagon pulled up to the back of the store, as she rushed to see who was driving the wagon, as the man who had delivered here the last month had caught her eye as none other ever had, and she had embarrassed the fellow as she caught him staring at her not once, but twice, she simply smiled at him, but it caught him off guard, as he didn't even realize that he was staring at her . . . After Mary saw that is was the same man, she went back to filling Mrs. Brown's dry goods from the barrels and gunnysacks. Mrs. Brown noticed at once that Mary was definitely pre-occupied with getting a second glance at the man . . . .

Mrs. Brown put her hand on Mary's arm and told her "Why honey, I can wait a spell, why don't you just go ask the man in for a cup of coffee, there is a chill in the air you know, it's not everyday you get to meet a fine looking fellow around here and I wouldn't mind getting a glimpse of the fellow either by the way he has taken your attention, what's the mans name honey"?

Mary slightly flushed of the face: "Mrs. Brown, I don't rightly know his name, I only met him the one time about a month ago" . . .

Mrs. Brown simply smiles at Mary and walks to the back door, "Young fella, you need to step in here and catch a breath and have a sip of some fine hot coffee, and could I ask you to assist me in getting my things loaded onto my buckboard"?

Mrs. Brown was a farm-raised woman. A healthy fifty years of age, with skin tanned from working side by side with her husband of thirty years . . . There wasn't an ounce of fat on the woman; you could tell she had done more than her share of hard work . . . . It was simple to see, she needed help from no one . . .

Wade was an observant man, but women were a total mystery to him, he knew little of their ways or thoughts, and they made him way more nervous than men did . . . But he knew he was anxious to return here to this town, he had asked for this delivery, because he remembered the lady that worked here . . .

Mary Franks was a fine looking woman, a tall slender woman with long dark hair and blue eyes, when her eyes met Wades, he felt like she could see right into his heart . . . Wade remembered how she made him feel so warm the last time, a feeling he had not experienced before . . . Little did Wade know, she had felt that same way about him . . .

Wade had gestured to Mrs. Brown that he would be in shortly . . . And then he went about taking care of his team, checking their feet and talking to them as if they knew every word he was saying . . . Checking all the harnesses and re-adjusting here and there, stroking them on the neck as he finished his routine . . . Mary had been watching him all the time through the slightly distorted panes of glass of the back door. When he finished taking stock of his team he entered through the back door with freight papers in hand . . .

He had stepped through the door quietly enough that no one hardly noticed his presence, except Mary . . . And she had seen his every move . . . Wade had paused momentarily just after entering the room, stepping to the side not allowing the light of the windows to silhouette his frame and to allow his eyes to adjust to the different light and to observe all his surroundings of the room, he had been here before, but wanted to refresh the layout of the store room in his mind, something he had learned to rely his life on . . . Just as he remembered it, the store counter was on his left, the large plank floors that creaked as you stepped on them, the pot bellied stove was adjacent across the room, a tinge of wood smoke drifted in the air and a warmth that goes with a fire, the front door in front of him and a window on each side of the door . . . Barrels of dry goods and bolts of materials for the women stood to the right, in the rear of the room stood shovels and axes and tools required for living in the wilds of the area . . . Wade also picked up the smells of tobacco and freshly ground coffee . . .

Wade took a further step into the room, "I don't mind if I do take you up on that fresh coffee if you've got some left" . . .

Mrs. Brown looked at Mary who was standing there half in a daze . . . "Mary, you gonna get this fella some coffee or does he have to wait on himself"?

To which Mary replied, "He isn't helpless is he"? "Does he have a broken arm or something"? Wryly smiling as she talked . . .

But while she was talking she was making her way across the room, wearing a chambray leather colored skirt drawn tightly around her waist with a black belt and a tucked in white shirt, laced up boots just above her ankles, her sleeves were rolled back halfway between her elbow and her wrist, she had picked up a granite coffee mug from behind the counter, a man sized mug with a good sturdy handle on the side, she walked gracefully across the plank floor to the wood stove and picked up the granite pot and pours a steaming hot cup of coffee, and while she stands there she opens the door of the stove and pitches in a couple of sticks of wood on the fire. She hands Wade the cup, he reaches out his hand to take it, wearing a leather drovers glove worn from use, Mary pauses for a second before handing it over and he realizes his gloves are still on, and he quickly removes them, stashing them in his coat pockets . . .

Mrs. Brown picks up her sack of goods and heads for the door, Wade rushing over to help her . . . "Ma'am, I thought you needed help loading your supplies"?

Mrs. Brown simply smiles back at Wade. "I was mistaken, I can handle this just fine, I think maybe you will be the one needing help young man" . . .

Wade just had a puzzled look on his face as he doesn't get what just whizzed over his head . . . and takes a deep sip of the coffee, which tasted as good as it smelt . . . Refreshing and warm . . . Warm as it went down and warm to the touch of his hands as he cradles the cup with both hands . . .

Mary was watching every move he made, observing and analyzing his every move, Wade had already sized the room in his own eyes, he knew where everyone in the store was standing, he knew none of them, but had realized he had drawn all of their attention, a few had picked up what they came for and scurried on out the door.

Wade broke the silence: "Did I hear the lady calling you Mary?

"Yes you did sir, it would be Mary Franks, Ms. Mary Franks" . . .

Wade did catch the Ms. in the statement, and it made a warm feeling in him that he didn't really understand why . . . But deep inside, it was something he wanted to hear . . .

"Well Mary Franks, where would you like me to unload your wagon of goods, there is quite a load of different things" . . .

Mary knew exactly where Mr. Roberts would want them unloaded but instead said: "Well I am not sure of where Mr. Roberts would like them, he should be back within the hour, can you wait for him"?

"I don't reckon I'm going anywhere for the time being, it will be too late in the day for me to head back out, I sort of thought I'd like a room and a hot bath tonight, I've been sleeping under that wagon long enough."

Mary smiled at him, which gave him an even warmer feel than the coffee did . . ." Well sir, you know my name but I can't say the same for you" . . .

Wade swirled the last sip of coffee around in his mouth getting the last taste of it before swallowing it, and stated: "Ma'am the name would be Wade, Wade Tavner" . . .

A short stocky man that had been over at the far end of the counter, weighing out some spike nails, stepped up abruptly, "I've heard that name before, I heard them say you shot down a couple men over in Ft. Laramie awhile back, shot em out right, and one of them was already holding a gun on you . . . They say you were real fast and a killing type of a man" . . . .

Wade gave the man a look, disgusted at the situation, but simply replied, "Ahh you know better than to believe rumors and gossip like that, they say Jesse James shot and killed a hundred men, you know that ain't true" . . . Hoping that would end this conversation . . . He had nothing to hide, but didn't want this to be the topic of discussion . . . Luckily the man's wife was ready to leave, so after paying their tab, they left out the front door, as Wade watched them through the front window, as they climbed into a buckboard with a thin chested gaited horse and trotted on down the main street of town . . .

Wade looked over to Mary, who was acting to be busy with re-arranging bolts of materials . . . "I guess I should step out and tend my wagon until Mr. Roberts shows up" . . .

"Nonsense Mr. Tavner, you just stay put, I could fix you a bit of grub if you like, we have some meats and bread in back for sandwiches, you must be hungry from your long ride getting here" . . .

"Well Ma'am, I couldn't ask you for that, I had some jerky on the way up just a bit ago, I ain't likely to starve to death" . . .

"Mr. Tavner, I'd prefer it if you called me Mary and not ma'am" as she smiled at him again . . .

"Then my name would be Wade to you too ma'am, I mean Mary" . . .

"Wade I intend to fix myself something to eat, and I would prefer not to eat alone and Aunt Martha didn't raise me to be impolite, so I would take it as a favor if you would let me fix you a bite too" . . . Mary fixed him the best roast beef sandwich he had ever had in his life, he would have loved to had another one, but was embarrassed to ask, he feared he had ate the first one like a starved dog . . . Mary had carved off a chunk of cheese from a big round block that set on the back shelf of the store, and Wade washed it all down with another cup of the fresh coffee that set on the stove . . .

Mary emptied the last of the pot and walked to the counter and grabbed a handful of coffee beans from a burlap bag behind the counter and walked to the grinder and dropped them in and turned the handle a few quick rounds, the fresh ground coffee had a warm smell that quickly filled the room, as she walked back to the pot and filled it with water and the fresh ground coffee and returned it to the stove . . . Wade had watched every move she had made, and unknowingly to himself, was smiling all the time . . .

Bill and Martha Roberts returned to the store and entered through the front door. They were a friendly couple. Bill was a short stocky built fella with big forearms and wide shoulders, a bit of a belly that protruded out past his belt . . . Martha was about the same height as Bill was, with reddish brown hair, just short of her shoulders but pulled back and tied with a strip of cloth that had blue flowers on it . . . Bill and Martha were Mary's aunt and uncle . . . Her father had sent her here when she was five years old . . . Her mother had died when she was only two, and her father felt he couldn't raise her properly, the Roberts had no family of their own and had raised Mary as such . . . They were the only parents Mary knew . . . Mary grew up in Ft. Douglas, all the merchants on the main street knew Mary well and thought the best of her. They too, had seen her grow up in their town from a little girl to the fine lady she was now . . .

Wade stepped up to Mr. Roberts and retrieved the freight papers from the inside of his coat pocket. Wade stuck out his right hand for a friendly handshake with the papers in his left hand . . . Then asked where he would like his goods unloaded . . .

Bill simply said: "Well we'll put the dry goods in the store room and the hardware items in the utility shed out back, didn't Mary tell you where?"

"Well sir, Mary said she wasn't sure where you would want them" . . . .

Martha quickly glanced at Mary and gave her a sly look and winked at her . . . She had already noticed the two dirty dishes and two cups setting on the edge of the counter and had already assumed what had taken place here . . . . She had approved, Wade was a good looking man in her eyes too . . . And he seemed to be a good honest man . . .

Wade went about his chores of unloading the wagon, stacking the small barrels in neat rows along the back wall and packing in the gunny sacks loaded with wheat, the Roberts ground their own flour and meal here in the store and repackaged it for resale to their patrons . . . All the while Wade was going about his work, Mary couldn't help but watch his every move . . .

Martha had noticed that Mary couldn't keep her eyes on her own chores of the store, and more than that, Martha could see a different look in Mary's eyes that she hadn't ever seen before . . . Martha knew what that look meant . . . She approached Wade, "Young man, if you have no plans for supper tonight, we would be appreciative to have you eat with us in our home to show our gratitude for the work you have done for us" . . .

Martha had a warm smile to her face. Wade stepped up taking his gloves back off and unbuttoned his jacket . . . "Ma'am, I couldn't impose on you like that, I've just been doing my job" . . .

"Nonsense, you wouldn't be imposing on anybody, I'll be fixing supper for the rest of us anyway and there will be plenty for you too . . . Our house is the third one on the east side of town as you came in, we will be expecting you, we would greatly appreciate your company and maybe hear some news from the rest of the world . . . Supper will be served at seven o'clock sharp . . . Don't be late" and she turned around and walked away not leaving time for Wade to refuse . . .

That almost sounded like an order, so how could he refuse . . . "Yes Ma'am, I would not be late and have thick gravy" . . .

"And what would make you think you were having any gravy tonight young man"?

Wade smiled: "Just wishing I guess Ma'am" . . . As he walked out the door towards his team, but he glanced back inside the door as he left to see Mary standing there watching him leave, she smiled as he nodded his head and tipped his hat to her . . .

Wade drove his team down to the livery stables and bedded them down and gave them a bucket of oats, then proceeded to brush them out paying extra care where the harness wears on them, making sure of no sores . . . They were good horses, Wade had picked them out himself . . . After finishing up with his team, Wade strolled down the street towards Charlie Benton's Hotel . . . He walked past the general store on his way and let his eye wander inside the store and saw Mary watching him walk by, he acted as though he didn't notice, but when he stopped in front of the hotel he peered back over his shoulder and saw Mary peering out through the cracked door . . . Wade walked on in and paid two bits for a room . . .

Charlie Benton was behind the desk and tossed him a key to room seven, "Up the stairs to the left, third door down, it better be quiet by nine o'clock, I don't tolerate no nonsense either" . . . .

"Not a problem sir, what's the chances of getting a hot bath around town"?

"Got a back room right here with a hot bath, that'll be another nickel though and it won't be ready for another hour or so" . . .

"I'll take it" . . . As Wade digs out another five cent piece and tosses it to him . . . Charlie tosses it back, "Pay the lady back there, it's her job not mine" . . .

Wade climbs the steps which are steep and narrow and the boards creak as you step higher, a condition which he liked though. He liked the sound of boards creaking as you stepped on them, just like a good rocking chair should creak too . . . Plus it also made it difficult to be slipped up on, Wade was always an extremely cautious man . . .

The room was quaint and small, but efficient enough for what he wanted . . . To his right was a wardrobe to which a person could hang a few clothes, a drawer which had a couple of clean towels folded neatly, to the left of the door set a wash stand with a pitcher and bowl for cleaning up, and it had a mirror attached to the back, the mirror was spotted and not to clear, but the man looking back at him in it seemed dirty and needed a good cleaning up, he had thought of how Mary had seen him . . . The bed was straight ahead in front of the door, which had a clean white quilt laid on top with big soft feather pillows . . . Wade just smiled at himself, as he hadn't slept on a pillow and a clean bed in some time . . .

After a short rest in the room Wade ventured down the stairs to the back room and treated himself to a hot bath . . . The water was clean and so hot, it was hard to get in, he had to ease into it a little at a time . . . A heavy set woman walked around the partition that was standing there and asked for her five cents . . . Wade quickly made it into the hot water with ease, then asked her to hand his pants over, he reached into the pocket and retrieved the money for her, as he stayed slid way down into the water . . .

She just smiled: "Mister, you ain't going to embarrass me none"

"Well Ma'am, I can't rightly say the same thing" . . . She gave a deep laugh as she left the room, as Wade was the only customer in there at the time . . .

The hot bath felt good, it felt good to be clean, it had been a month since Wade had taken a hot bath, he cleaned regularly, but out on the trail in cold streams . . . He borrowed a pair of scissors and trimmed his beard up, as it had grown straggly too . . . Another look in the mirror and he could see some improvements, but felt he was way out of his class thinking of Mary Franks . . .

Wade had returned to his room and lay stretched out on the bed, it was soft as the feather mattress encompassed around his body . . . He was tired and it felt good to be refreshed . . . He hadn't spent very many a night in a soft bed . . . Afraid to relax too much though, as he didn't want to be late for his invitation for supper . . . Wade closely watched his watch, as time seemed to crawl by, finally it read a quarter to seven . . . He hitched his holster back up and tied it low to his leg, he had considered not wearing it, but that thought was quickly dismissed, maybe he could wear it tied higher up as wearing a holster tied low was a sure sign of trouble as men who considered themselves gun slingers wore them tied so low, but Wade had tried to wear it high like most ranchers and farmers did but just couldn't get used to the feel of it there, and it was terribly unhandy wearing a gun strapped so high on a man's waist . . . This was him, if these folks disapproved, then so be it . . .

Wade strolled down the boardwalk towards the Roberts home, aware of every move and shadow that presented itself along the main street, nothing went unnoticed and he took great pride in that fact, he had learned to trust his life to it, but he never looked like he was studying his surroundings . . .

Wade stepped up on the front porch of the Roberts home, the front porch had a swing attached to the roof of the overhang which gave a view of the main street and across the street there was an opening that you could see out into the valley that stretched out into the distant horizon, the sun was setting low and cast shadows from across the street that reached to the front of the house . . . The house was painted white and flowers lined the walk to the porch, he could smell scents of the flowers and also of the food being cooked within the house . . . This was a home, something he hadn't seen much of in his life, he remembered slightly what it was like when he was a young boy, theirs was nothing like this, their house had no paint and no flowers, but it seemed he could still smell his mom's cooking and the warmth that went with a house being a home . . .

After pausing momentarily he took another step towards the door, the wood planks on the porch creaked as he stepped, making him cringe slightly as he always walked with as much caution as possible . . . Mary stepped to the door before he had time to knock, and opened it wide for him to enter . . . "Wade, I am so glad you decided to join us, I have looked forward to seeing you again all afternoon" . . .

Wade couldn't help but smile back as he looked into her blue eyes that seemed to be the prettiest thing he'd ever seen before, and her smile just warmed him throughout his entire body . . . Mary had changed her clothes also and had combed her hair down, it had always been pulled back in a pony tail every other time he had seen her, her dark colored hair flowed just past her shoulders and lay beautiful naturally, a few locks that dropped in front of her shoulders and the rest hung down behind her shoulders down her back, the locks that laid down the front, softly encompassed her face, she had on a black stone necklace that also highlighted her dark hair and accented the features of her face, not that anything needed any help, she was a fine looking woman . . . She was wearing a white shirt with some lace placed in all the right places with a black skirt that fit neatly to her waist and laced up boots, riding boots . . .

He could hardly speak as he was not used to this sort of thing, "I am glad to be here, I am appreciative that you folks would even ask me to share a meal with you" . . .

Wade stepped in the door and quickly removed his hat and ran his fingers through the thick black hair trying to arrange it as best he could, he fumbled with his holster and removed it also, the last thing he wanted to do was scratch the nice chairs Mrs. Roberts had in her home . . . There was a hall tree close by the door and he hung his hat and holster on it . . . He wore a leather vest that fit neatly to his chest and waist, a tanned smooth leather vest with a denim shirt underneath it and black denim jeans with boots that showed signs of several years of wear . . .

At first he felt very uncomfortable, but the Roberts quickly made him feel right at home, as conversation at the table was good . . . Bill Roberts was a man interested in the goings on in the public arena of politics . . . Although he had no desire of running for any office of his own, but this was a new country and politics were starting to play a role in what went on out here in the west . . . Up to now, this part of this great land had no laws except what the folks here set forth . . .

The meal was one of the finest Wade had ever ate, fried chicken and mashed tators with gravy and fresh biscuits straight from the wood stove that crackled in the kitchen, there was fresh honey still with the comb in it and fresh churned butter for the hot biscuits . . . Afterwards, a peach cobbler was offered . . . Wade had tried not to eat like a starved wolf, he didn't want to embarrass himself, but he did ask for a second helping of the cobbler . . . Martha Roberts liked to see a man eat good, as most women do it seemed . . .

After the meal, the conversation was moved to the parlor room where Bill Roberts pulled out a pipe and stoked it with a dark leafy tobacco, the smell did linger in the air and smelt good, Bill had offered a pipe to Wade, but he refused as he cared not to smoke . . .

An hour of conversation and Wade felt it was time for him to leave as he didn't want to wear out his welcome, but deep inside he was enjoying the company immensely . . . This was a good family that enjoyed life just as it was . . . Wade lifted his watch from his vest pocket and it read nearly nine o'clock, and used the excuse that he needed to be up early to head out with his team . . . The moon had replaced the sun with dim light as he stepped out on the porch, Mary had followed him out the door and shut the door behind her . . . Mary wasn't ready for him to leave, and she was convinced he never needed to go . . . She gave him the invitation to set on the swing for a spell and view the moon with her . . . It was a beautiful night, clear as fine crystal, only the slightest breeze which felt good to the face as it drifted by . . . Wade accepted the invitation with great gratitude, as deep down, he didn't want to leave either . . .

After an hour of setting on the swing Wade got up: "Mary, I must go, it would not be good for me to be here any longer with you, you make me feel like never leaving, I have had a wonderful evening with you and your family" . . . but lingered, like he wanted to say more, but instead turned towards the steps . . .

Mary followed to the steps, just as his foot was about to leave the porch platform she reached out and grabbed his right arm which turned him slightly towards her, she quickly leaned over and gave him a kiss on the cheek and a hug, his arm slid around behind her back and pulled her close and held her tight for just an instant, as Mary turned and went back to the door . . . "I wish to see you again Mr. Wade Tavner" . . .

Mary walked back in the door of the house as Wade stumbled down the remaining two steps, he had never felt like this before . . . He entered the hotel room realizing he didn't even know that he had walked down the street, he could have been run over by a walking horse . . .

The bed had felt good, but Wade didn't sleep well during the night . . . He rose before the sun did, quickly rinsed water across his face and stretched out his muscles which seemed tired . . . Slapped on his boots and holster and headed to the livery stable . . . He needed to be out on the trail with his team of fine horses . . . Wade walked past the Roberts general store on his way and peeked inside, the door still locked but Bill Roberts was in the back cleaning, he quickly walked on, but heard the door open behind him, Bill Roberts hollered at him, Wade turned to face him, he was standing there with a white canvas apron tied around his waist holding a broom for which he started sweeping the boardwalk in front of the store, "Mary was hoping to see you before you left, she will be here at the store directly or you can stop at the house if you would like" as he simply smiled and went about his business . . .

Wade continued on to the livery stable to tend his horses, he went about his daily chores of caring for his team which he did with precise intent, checking the horses as well as all the harness, making any adjustments that needed to be done . . .

He noticed a horse in the third stall as you walked in the stable, a horse alert to his surroundings, ears erect, eyes alert and sharp, a horse with some fire to him, Wade walked over closer to the horse and was admiring the animal when the ole stable hand walked up . . . An older man of good age and wisdom to boot, a man who had been around good horse flesh all his life,

"He's a fine animal, right fine, but he's a one person horse, he's all fired up till Ms. Mary brings him out of that stall and saddles him up, then he's like a kids pony, but he sure ain't like that for me, ornery old fart" . . .

"So he belongs to Mary Franks does he?"

"Yes sir he does, and she can ride too, don't ride like a woman, she can ride as good as any man I ever been around, she's good with animals" . . . .

Wade went back to his team, he was nearly harnessed up and ready to leave, wondering if he should stop in and holler at her or just head on out, he started to have an uncomfortable feel about the whole thing, his mind felt uneasy and boggled up, as though he couldn't think straight . . .

A voice interrupted his thoughts, it was the voice of Mary Franks, she walked gracefully into the stables . . . "Uncle Bill said you had stopped by early this morning, were you going to tell me something? Will you be back soon"?

His thoughts seemed to really boggle his throat even more now, but Wade managed a smile and words fell out that he didn't even realize he was thinking . . . "I'm afraid you'd get tired of seeing me too much if I had the chance" . . .

"Well sir, I don't see that being a problem" . . .

"Mary, I will be back, and I hope it won't be long" . . .

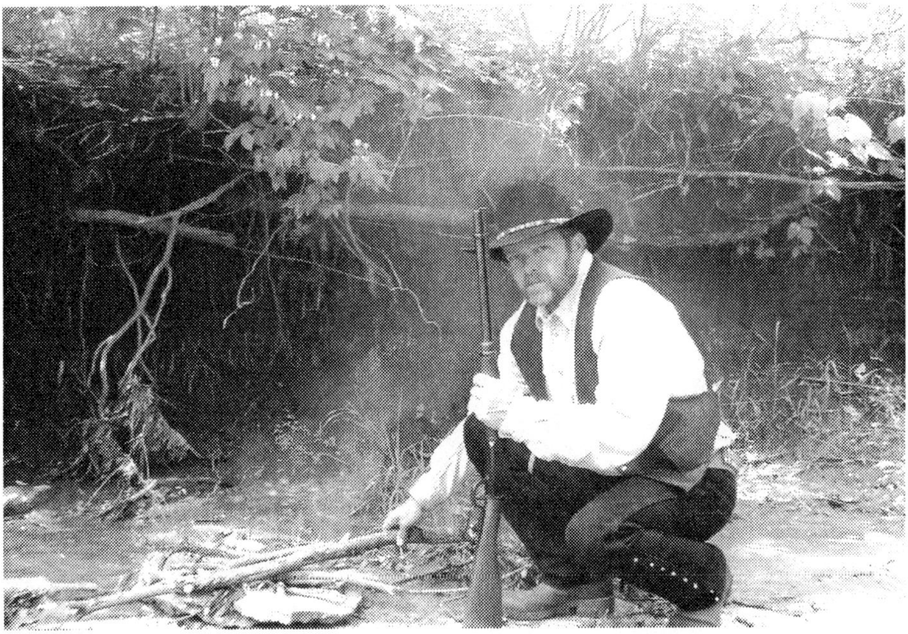

Chapter 3

Wade headed his wagon into the street and turned south, the livery stable was at the north end of town, he kicked the team into a good pace moving out down main street, he gave a good hard look at the general store as he passed by, Mary and her Aunt Martha were both standing at the front door, Mary raised her hand and gave him a wave, but her eyes seemed to beckon to him, Wade simply nodded his head and touched the tip of his hat brim with his hand as the team stretched out on down the lane, the horses were well rested and fed and eager to be moving out . . . Wade felt this would be a long ride back to Denver . . . He swung his team into the sawmill that was set up about two miles south of town . . . He was to pick up a load of ten foot planks to haul back and to peddle them to the small towns that were popping up in the plains areas between Ft. Douglas and Denver . . . These small towns in the high plains were hard pressed for good lumber, so Wade could make a few dollars peddling lumber on his way back . . .

He was hoping to get it sold and unloaded at some of the first few towns, he could get an empty wagon back quicker as the horses could move out faster and last longer, Wade knew the limits of his team, and he planned to push them to that limit, he would in no way over work them, but he wanted to get back as soon as he could . . . He had things to do . . .

Setting on the porch swing with Mary last night, he determined his future . . . Wade had told Mary of the valley he had found and described it in such accurate detail, that she felt like she could nearly see it . . . He had told Mary that he wanted to homestead there and settle it and raise cattle and some of the finest horses in the country, that was his dream . . . Mary's comment to him was simple . . . "What's stopping you? There's no one stopping you but you yourself . . . You should do it" . . . Wade knew she was right, and there was no better time than the present . . .

Wade stopped at Sweet Springs and had the luck to sell all his lumber at the first stop . . . He had to deliver it a few miles out of town . . . A man building a shanty of a cabin with plank siding, rough sewn, not more than fourteen feet in both directions, a window on two sides that could be boarded shut in minutes and a slat door on the front, a few rough pieces of hand crafted furniture, a well was already dug close by for water, the water was cool and had a fresh taste to it as Wade lifted the dipper to his mouth and drank his fill, and then took a couple of buckets of the fresh water to his horses, they drank deep for a few minutes and then Wade pulled the buckets away from them and made them wait a few minutes before giving them the rest, for giving a hot horse to much cold water at once can make them sick . . . It was getting late in the afternoon and the man offered to let Wade stay the night here, but Wade could see a few more hours on the trail to home, so now with an empty wagon he figured he could make good time . . .

Two weeks later Wade Tavner pulled into Mcnall's Freight Company, Roger Mcnall stepped out to greet his best driver and good friend . . . Roger had become to rely on Wade for many tasks around the place, whenever he needed more horse flesh he always sent Wade or went along with Wade, for he knew horseflesh better than any person he'd ever met, and Wade had never brought a shavetail back, all of his buys were good horses, good solid animals, animals ready for the work loads . . .

Wade climbed down from his wagon to greet Roger Mcnall, Wade had a somber look on his face . . . Roger stuck out his hand with a smile: "It's good to see you back Wade, I've got a special load that needs to be in New Mexico as soon as we can get it there, I was afraid you weren't going to get here in time to take it, it's a priority load and needs special attention to get there, it will pay you double your wages to make it by the first of the month" . . .

"I'm sorry Roger, you'll have to get Lonnie or Steve Wilmot, they are both good drivers and dependable . . . I came to collect my wages and my horse, it's time for me to get on with my life" . . .

"Wade, is there something wrong"?

"No Roger, NO, everything is right, it's time for me to move on, I have valued you as a true friend for now and for always, but I must do what I must do" . . .

Wade walked into the office with Roger and picked up his pay and shook hands, Roger had stuck a little extra pay in the brown envelope and handed it to Wade, he didn't count it as he trusted his boss with his own life . . . "Wade, can I ask what it is you plan to do"?

"I'm going to homestead that valley I'd told you about, I'm going to make something of it or die trying, if you're ever up that way, stop in and give me some help" . . . Wade stuffed the envelope inside his coat pocket and walked on down to the stables owned by Mcnall where his own mount was stalled, he was a beautiful horse of a good fifteen hands and maybe a little more, solid built, strong muscular hind quarters and a thick chest, his neck flowed into his body with elegance, nothing out of proportion, a good wide stance between his feet . . . Wade brushed off his back and tossed the saddle pad on and then hoisted his hand made roping saddle on top, nothing fancy about the saddle, very little tooling, just a good solid saddle of good leather and a strong tree . . . He gathered up the rest of his gear and headed out . . . Roger wanted to try to talk him out of leaving and get him to stay, but he knew that would be fruitless, for he knew Wade Tavner's mind was made up and set, there would be no changing of that . . .

It was mid afternoon already, but he was in a hurry to get going, his first stop would be on the edge of town at Laudlands Law Office, where he intended to file his claim legal and all . . . After some time of viewing maps, a legal description was penned out and laid claim on, Jack Laudland had been around the area for years, he was one of the first in Denver to set up office and knew the legal aspects of staking a claim . . . He assured Wade that it would be recorded in the US Government Offices and filed tomorrow, and he told Wade, not to worry, "You ain't likely to run into anyone else up there wanting to dispute your claim on that piece of ground, hell, you're probably the only man who knows it exist, if I was you I'd stake out whatever else I wanted when you get there" . . .

Wade walked out feeling like a kid, his chest felt a size bigger, and he was surprised his hat still fit, he'd never felt so proud of himself than he did at this moment in time . . . He swung up on the big sorrel gelding and reigned him around to the north . . . He would have to travel north for some distance before turning back west, there were tall steep mountain ranges west of Denver and could only be crossed in certain places, there were places in these ranges that stayed snow packed even during the summer months, a few days ride north and the higher peaks leveled off some and the passes easier to navigate, but even there it would take days to reach the other side, once on the other side you were in the high plateaus that reached into the horizon with big open valleys that held tremendous herds of buffalo and large amounts of elk and mule deer, bears were numerous in some areas too . . .

The sun was setting low in the western horizon as Wade rode into a patch of cottonwood trees with a few pine trees mingled in down along the Platte River, dark would soon settle in, for when the sun reached the tops of the peaks, it disappeared quickly and most nights the temperatures would drop with the sun . . . Camp was set up with a good fire of pine limbs broken off the lower portion of the trees where the limbs had died out from lack of sunshine from the higher limbs, a two inch thick dead pine limb made a good fire and very little smoke, not until the fire had died down and the red coals remained, did

Wade start to fix his supper, he didn't realize how hungry he had become until he started to smell his food cooking, he had shot a rabbit back an hour before setting up camp and he always carried a small skillet when traveling, he had sliced off a hunk of slab bacon and rolled it in the skillet and got it greased and seasoned good before throwing the young rabbit in, between the smell of wood burning and the bacon grease and the rabbit searing, it was enough to make a man weak, he had brought a small bag of sourdough biscuits and tore one in half and ate with the rabbit and then finished off the other half as well . . . With a full belly and the fire kindled back up to a good blaze, Wade settled down for a good nights rest, but his mind was running full speed of his new direction that he had chosen to send his life, being excited was an understatement, his thoughts would run from the valley in which he was headed, back to the evening spent setting on the porch with Mary Franks . . . Little did he know, that Mary Franks was thinking of him as well . . .

Morning rolled in with the promise of a fine day, the sun was trying to peak into the new day from the eastern horizon, a thin thread of distant clouds to the east made the sun cast a red tint in the sky . . . Wade was up and had his fire going well before the sun broke the morning skyline, a fresh cup of boiled coffee, he never carried a pot, he always boiled the grounds straight in his cup, drink it down to the bottom quarter inch and toss the grounds on the fire . . . The sun was casting light on the top of the mountain ranges to the west, "Time to head out big fella" he told his big sorrel, and it seemed as though the horse knew all to well what Wade had just said, saddled and cinch tight, bedroll rolled and strapped to the back of the saddle and any signs of camp being removed, Wade stepped into the saddle and headed the sorrel north and west, there was a good pass up the Poudre River and canyons, it was a steep pass and rough going, little used, with some of the best scenery in the country, most travelers used the trails south of here, but Wade's valley lay well north of those passes . . . The sorrel was feeling rested from staying well fed back at Mcnall's stables and was eager to be out, so Wade gave him his head with slack reigns and the big horse took the invitation to put some ground under his belly, it was as though he was as excited about being out as his rider and owner was . . .

Heading west and north up Poudre River the travel got tough, the waters were still running high this year from a good snow of last winter and the terrain was rocky and steep, thinking of making good time would be futile, to hurry would result in a lame horse or worse . . . The pines grew tall and thick and the undergrowth was thick and green . . . Following close to the river was the best course, a man who thinks he can cut course and pick up time in these mountains is fooling himself, you can get lost or get trapped in box canyons that can make you back track for days . . . The water that flows in these rivers is coming from the top of the snow covered peaks and they have cut the trail for you to follow, at times there are a lot of switchbacks that you can cut a new swath, but then to get out in the open flats and get tangled in beaver runs and the such can wear a man and horse down . . .

After days of following the river Wade reached the peaks of this range, setting his horse atop the peaks, a man could see for eternity it seemed, it was mind boggling to look out into such a vastness of territory, it was awesome to see such a country laid out in front of you like it was, the trees were such a dark green that they nearly looked blue in the afternoon sun, words cannot describe the beauty and vastness that lay ahead of him . . . The day was winding down as the sun was reaching the far horizon, the sun was casting long shadows from where Wade set his horse . . . As he set above the timberline taking in the depths of his view, he realized how lucky he was to be out here, the air was fresh and crisp, the scent of pines floated in the air, he would ride back down below tree line to set camp . . . The winds can pick up high on the peaks and the temperatures could drop to freezing on the warmest of summer days here, a man didn't want to set camp above the trees as protection from the elements of mother nature up here were nil . . . The sun had set as Wade finished setting up his camp, elk and mule deer roamed out freely in the short grasses that supported these high meadows . . . Wade staked his sorrel close to a small stream where the grass seemed taller and fresher and the big fella seemed grateful as he bit off clumps of the grass, Wade smiled to himself as he set there leaned up against a log in his camp, he could hear the big sorrel chewing the grass in his teeth, and occasionally stretching and blowing through his nostrils . . . Nighttime arrived quickly and the sounds that floated on the air changed to that of coyotes and the howling of wolves with an occasional hoot of an owl or the wisp of wings of the night birds that catch bugs drifting in the cool night air . . . Wade always knew the sounds that were around him, and always knew what sounds should be around him, and was even more aware when those sounds weren't there, animals were scarce and quiet during signs of danger, so deathly quiet was a sure sign of danger or something out of the normal in the woods . . . All seemed good as the evening sounds were typical of what he wanted to hear and his eyes became heavy with sleep . . . Sleep hadn't come easy since leaving Ft. Douglas for he couldn't get thoughts of Mary Franks from taking over his mind, giving him a troubled feeling . . . Something inside of him told him to head back to Ft. Douglas and visit more with her, but his better judgment told him to push on to the valley, a woman as pretty as that wouldn't want to come out in this wilderness and face the dangers and toils of this kind of life . . . It wouldn't even be fair to ask her to leave the home she had, their home was a real home, warm and secure, clean and proper, there was always food to eat, a bed to sleep in, a dry bed in rainy weather, no, this was no life for a woman so fine . . .

Waking early the next morning, Wade could feel a dampness in the air, his bones felt tired and stiff this morning from riding in hard country then sleeping on the ground all night, and it seemed the temperatures had gotten down to near freezing, there were no shickles of ice in his coffee mug, but he felt it must be close to freezing temperatures, he dug out his coat that was rolled up in his bedroll and pulled it on, the sky was gray, darker than normal, he pulled out his pocket watch and it read six thirty of the morning, standing and stretching to loosen up his muscles and to get the blood flowing he looked out into the west, there lay a bank of clouds dark of color, and the lighter it got around him, the darker the clouds seemed to get, and they were approaching fast . . . Storms rolled in quickly in the mountains as they rolled across the high plains building as they moved . . . Wade quickly pulled up camp, knowing how violent storms can get at this altitude and saddled the sorrel and headed him down the face of the mountain heading towards the approaching storm, he was trying to make time, he was looking for some form of shelter to get in and out of danger, he had seen storms like this before . . . Switching back around a sharp bend of rocks he spotted an overhang above him, the rocks protruded out a good fifteen feet from the base, turning the sorrel and heading him up towards it, rain had already started to pelt down and the slope was wet and slick, but this sorrel was a mountain bred animal and dug in deep and pushed with the strong hind quarters and leveled off in front of the overhang, plenty of room for Wade and his horse, Wade instinctively started hauling wood in under the shelter, for you never knew how long it would take for a blue northerner to blow out . . . He set his cup under a lip of the rocks where water was dripping off, it would be filled quickly as he set about chopping off clumps of the grass with his knife for his companion . . . Only after caring for the sorrel did he pull back into the overhang and settle down himself, this could be a long day, or a couple of days, but he had all he needed here, soon a fire was kindled and a blaze boiling the cup of water with a pinch of grounds thrown in . . . This was a lonely life, the only way he knew it, and the only way he thought he wanted it, but felt a call within his body that waned of something with more substance, feelings he'd never felt before . . . Feelings for a companion, other than his horse, a woman, were growing stronger with every heartbeat, not just any woman, because none had ever affected him like Mary Franks had . . . Wade fell asleep in the middle of the day with thoughts of setting on the porch swing, with the sounds of rain pelting down on the leaves of the plants around his makeshift home for the time being, and the sound of his horse chewing grass . . .

Wade woke up and lifted his watch from his vest pocket, it was two in the afternoon, rain still falling lightly around, but they were still dry within their shelter, the rain had let up, so He led the sorrel down the slope to a small waterhole and let him drink his fill and walked him back, looking out towards the west, the sky was clearing off, "another hour or so big fella, no need getting soaked yet" . . . Wade stepped away and looked back towards the sorrel, wondering how many times he'd talked to his horse and never got an answer . . .

The late afternoon sun was peaking through the remnants of the storm that had blown in, saddling back up they slid their way down the slope and hit the trail heading west, a few more hours of riding before dark, rested, the sorrel led out at a good pace . . .

It had been three weeks since leaving Denver, making time when possible, but it felt all worth it when Wade rode into his valley . . . He set his horse on the south end of the valley which lay stretched out before him, he couldn't even make out the trees at the north end, it was so far off, there was a pride that came over him like nothing he'd felt before, this was his, he had laid claim to it, and here he was, all because the most beautiful woman he'd ever met simply told him "why not do it" . . .

The valley was not more that a quarter mile wide at any one point with a stream that ran down the west side of the valley with granite cliffs standing guard just past the stream reaching straight up in most places, the stream flowed from the southwest corner of the valley and after exploring it, ran into another smaller valley probably a good half mile deep which was totally blocked off from entrance from anywhere but through the main valley floor because of the granite walls that surrounded the place, farther down the west side of the main valley was another high meadow that set nearly a thousand feet above the main valley floor, an open meadow of maybe a thousand acres with lush grass that was fed by the melting snows from the peaks above it . . . A beaver pond at the far end of it that held promise to some fine cutthroat trout . . . The stream seemed to be full of brook and rainbow trout as you could see them darting from the edges of the water and the grass that overhung the banks, the air seemed purer and fresher than any on earth . . . Wade made a big loop out into the valley having visions of cattle and great horseflesh roaming freely about . . . He set his horse in amazement at his surroundings and how he felt . . .

The sun had dropped below the granite walls and dark fell instantly it seemed, Wade had been here all afternoon, and it only seemed like he'd been here a few minutes, his mind racing with thoughts of where he wanted to build his home, he wanted to sleep on this thought, there was plenty of time to beat the winter months yet, he wanted to figure every angle, from the warmest of winter and the coolest breezes for summer, where would the sun shine, where would block the harsh winter winds and where would the snow drift, all things he had learned in his two years of living in Montana, he didn't want to make the same mistakes that some of them did . . .

Wade was well awake an hour before the sun cast a shadow in his valley, he had already kindled his fire back into a blaze and had his coffee as well and a quick breakfast and as soon as it got daylight enough to see good, he saddled his sorrel and headed out into the valley to explore and discover where he would build his cabin . . . The sun was reaching near noon when Wade decided that building the cabin in the northwest corner of the valley was the proper thing to do, that was just below the high meadow and positioned on a knoll, not far from the stream so water would be an easy access, but high enough above the water so flood wouldn't be a concern, the cabin would be facing the south, there was a grove of aspens on the west side of the cabin which would block the heat of the afternoon sun in the summers, but the leaves would fall off in the fall allowing full sunshine during the colder months, the tall granite cliffs that lined the west side of the main valley floor would block any harsh winds from the north and west during the winter months, but an opening from the south would allow the cool summer breezes access to the cabin, the east side of the cabin would be pretty much open allowing the morning sun to reach through . . . He would work the rest of the day laying out his plans and marking what trees would be taken out and used and which ones should be left . . . Standing out in the valley, the cabin would be so nestled into the landscape that it would be hard to detect from sight . . .

Wade had heard that there was a mining town booming about twenty miles farther west of here, so he decided he could take a day of riding and buy some needed supplies and a few tools, he set down and made a list of what he would need for building his cabin . . . Tomorrow he would ride that way and see if he could locate it, it would be setting close to a river that flowed to the west from there . . .

Wade rode into Silver Creek Springs going on five o'clock, the only general store there was still open, the town wasn't much, most of it still living out of white canvas tents, but there were three saloons already, all serving out of the tent fashioned businesses, these towns boomed over night and sometimes disappeared as quickly as they sprang up . . . Ore and the thought of easy riches brought out the worst in people, and Wade wanted nothing to do with it, he had been to California a few years back and got a first hand look at the devastation it played on the mountains and streams, as clear streams turned brown and gray from the dirt and silt, and mountains were blasted away looking for the precious metals, in Wades eyes, no amount of money was worth that . . .

Wade bought a broad axe, a shovel, a one man crosscut, a brace and bit, a draw knife and a few smaller hand tools, it seemed that everyone he ran into was wanting to know where he was digging at . . . He had planned on staying the night in town, but decided he'd rather sleep out under the trees . . . A place like this was nothing more than trouble for a man wearing a low-slung colt . . . Wade strapped all his wares on the sorrel and headed out of town, apologizing to him for using him for a pack mule, and laughed to himself at what the sight of them must have looked like . . .

They rode a good three miles out of town with the last hour in the dark, this was no kind of country to be riding in the dark, but Wade wanted to be shy of town, he made a dry camp with no fire . . .

Wade entered his valley late in the day the next day as making time loaded with supplies was difficult to say the least, with just enough time to get things settled in, before dawn started creeping into his new home . . . Morning rolled around with a bright sun lifting above the horizon, a small mule deer buck had just walked out into the opening and Wade leveled off the sights on his 1866 Winchester and squeezed the trigger ever so slightly, the gun boomed and echoed down through the valley and off the granite walls, the deer took one jump towards the trees and folded up . . . Wade carefully skinned the animal with care of not cutting the hide, for he would be able to use it making things for the new cabin, he built his fire up and tossed on some bigger logs that he could keep burning all day and set up some green aspen limbs about an inch in diameter and hung strips of the deer meat above the smoke and fire, deer jerky was a good source of food, and he would need plenty stored up for the winter to come . . .

While keeping his fire going he also started cutting trees and dragging them to his cabin sight, when he had four good logs laid down he started to stack them in a square pattern with the two longer ones for the front and back, they were set on the ground then the two side logs were stacked on top, then marked where they laid and then rolled them back, then he took his broad axe and notched about half way down into the bottom logs then rolled them back into place, the foundation was laid . . .

The muscles in his arms and chest and back were tired, but a feeling that felt good . . . Tomorrow would be another day and he planned to lay maybe two more rows of logs, he wanted to lay them eight logs high to give plenty of head room inside, he'd been in some cabins where the builder quit a log or two short and a man of any height would have to duck his head to walk about . . . By the end of a week he had all the logs set and notched together and then started adding the roof with long poles, the poles were easier to handle because they were much smaller in diameter, once he got all the roof poles in place, he took his shovel to the north end of the valley where the granite walls played out, it was a damp place where springs sifted up through the ground and moss grew thick on the ground, Wade took his shovel and cut four foot square sections of the moss a good foot thick and hauled them back to the cabin and placed them on top of the poles of the roof, weaving sticks in and out of the moss to hold it in place, once it was all covered with moss, he fashioned a water bag from the deer hide and carried water and dowsed all the moss until it was thoroughly wet, a few times of doing this and the moss would grow back together and shed any rains that would fall . . .

The cabin was finished and looked good to his eye, it had a dirt floor, but he had spread pine needles throughout . . . With the drawknife he fashioned a bed with log rails and covered it with pine needles and a small layer of the moss then covered it with a piece of white canvas material that he had scrounged back at Silver Creek Springs . . . Night had fell once again, Wade slept good on his new bed, he felt it sure beat sleeping on the ground . . .

After a short breakfast, Wade picked up his ole iron skillet and tin plate he'd been eating out of and carried them to the stream behind the cabin, taking the skillet and scooping up some grit and sand at the waters edge he scoured them clean, the bottom side was blackened from cooking on the open fires and the bacon grease on the inside, dipping it back into the water and rinsing it out, something caught his eye, He swirled the water around again, gold flakes showed themselves in the bottom of his skillet . . . He quickly doused it back into the water, looking around to make sure no one had seen . . .

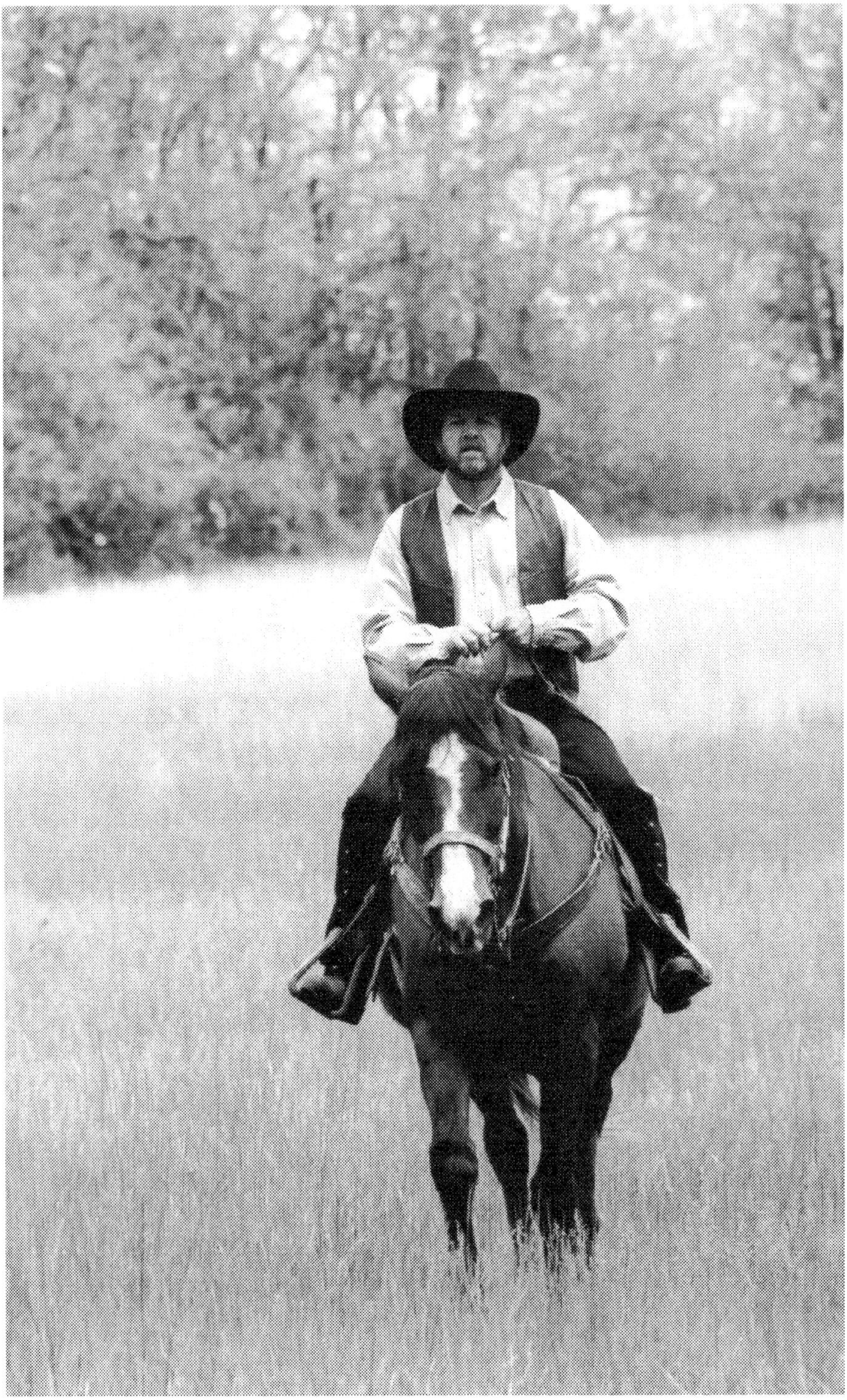

Chapter 4

The sun was getting close to late afternoon in Ft. Douglas . . . A couple of days earlier Bill Roberts had told Mary that they were expecting another load of freight and that is should be coming in anytime, he knew how much Mary wanted to see Wade Tavner again, and he had to admit, he liked the fella too, the man seemed quiet and to himself which wasn't a bad trait, but a man with an honest view of life and a man not afraid to stand for what was right, and he always conducted himself in a business like manner and showed no sign of fear of hard work . . . Bill had worried about the man's past, but then, no one was perfect, maybe he himself wasn't always the upstanding proprietor, but he did worry about the way Wade wore his gun slung low, if it wasn't trouble, it was an invitation to it . . . Martha had seen the way Mary had looked into the man's eyes, and she knew what that meant, she just didn't want to see her niece hurt, and she had also seen the same look in Wade's eyes looking at Mary . . .

Mary had come to work the last couple of days looking a little nicer than usual, she had no intention of Wade Tavner seeing her looking plain when he walked through that door, she had been leaving her hair down around her shoulders, and her dress kept clean and neat, other customers had come in and even made notice of how nice she looked, but she cared not of what others thought . . . The only compliment she wanted would have to come from Wade . . .

Every horse or wagon that rambled down the back alley caught Mary's attention and she made quick attention to the back door, but time and again, it wasn't Mcnalls Freight wagon . . .

Martha could feel the anticipation that Mary was going through as all mothers feel the hurt of their children . . . Bill and Martha were her uncle and aunt, but they had raised her as their own since she was five, and they were mom and dad . . .

It was nearly four o'clock in the afternoon when the wagon pulled up, Mary was filling an order, and all she could see was that it was Wade's team, they were a matching team of big strong horses, she was about to get beside herself trying to get the order filled, and about when she was finished, the man said: "Can ya fetch me some of them beans too, and weigh out some cracked flour along with em, about thirty pounds should do" . . . Well Mary would have to grind the flour as they kept wheat in barrels and ground it out fresh for customers . . . A look of disgust lined her face, but she started for the flour when Martha stepped over, "I'll finish this, you go see what's on the freight wagon to be unloaded" . . .

With a smile and a gleam in her eyes, Mary raced to the back door, to her surprise though, it was Steve Wilmot, setting the brake and tying off the reigns . . . Mary looked like someone had just tossed cold water on her . . . Steve Wilmot was a nice fellow, a talker, a likable sort of man, but not who she was looking for . . . Steve could see the disappointment in the look on Mary's face, "Ma'am, did I do something wrong"?

"Oh uh no . . . I, I mean we were expecting Mr. Tavner to bring this load, this will probably be the last load we receive before winter . . . Is Wade on another route or something"?

Steve hated to even say: "Well no ma'am, Wade up and pulled stakes last month, he rode into town and picked up his wages and all his belongings and headed out, they told me he was headed west, he just up and left ma'am, ain't none of us heard a word from him since" . . .

Mary's eyes became heavy and wet with tears as she stepped off the back steps and headed for the house at a run, Martha stepped out, and felt her pain deep in her own heart . . .

It was a pain Mary had not felt before, she felt like a part of her heart had just been cut out . . . Wade had not promised her anything, but she so wanted to see him again, and now, he was gone, without even saying a word . . . But the hurt wouldn't go away . . .

Bill and Martha finished the day at the general store and went home for the evening, supper was a quiet time tonight, Mary was short of conversation . . . Martha started to talk, thoughts of saying things like, there will be other young fellows to come along, she knew would not be what Mary would want to hear, so she kept quiet also . . . Bill talked of business matters and of the weather and of horses and who came in the store today and the such, as men do to avoid personal matters . . .

Wade Tavner had woke early and saddled his big sorrel gelding and rode out into his valley surveying what his next steps would be . . . Wade was a loner and had been for the most of his life, he had convinced himself, that was what he wanted, and that held true until as of late . . . Riding back to his cabin which looked like home, but it didn't feel like a home, there was something missing, and he knew what that something was, it was a companion, it was Mary Franks . . .

He wanted to pack up a few things and head back to Ft. Douglas, but that was a good hundred and fifty miles or more away, and after all, she had such a nice home where she was, far better than what he had to offer, she had nice clothes and numerous friends and her whole life was there in Ft. Douglas . . . He found a hundred good reasons not to go . . .

Another day and night had passed and all he could think of was Mary, so after several hours of deliberating against himself, Wade dug out his ole bedroll and duster and saddle bags and filled them with some of the jerky he'd dried and a few possibles he'd always carried, then saddled the big sorrel and headed north and east, he was going to pay her a visit . . . Test the waters . . .

It would take a few days to get back over the mountain ranges, but going farther north the mountains were not near as steep and rocky, then once out in the high plains he could make time, a good horse could cover a good thirty miles in a day, and he had as good a horse as there was . . . Getting out in the high plains presented many a sight, with the large herds of buffalo that roamed freely upon the prairie, with other herds of antelope, many a jack rabbit lay set in the edges of the brush and sage, the sky seemed to reach to eternity out here, sunsets always cast beautiful panoramic views that could last in a mans mind for eternity . . . He loved traveling and seeing this great country, he felt fortunate to live this life . . .

Wade had been on the trail for several days, it was late in the year and late summer months don't provide much rain out in the prairies, and he had ate several pounds of dust it seemed and his clothes showed it too . . . His hat brim was dusty with a sweat stained hatband, his clothes seemed to be saturated with the gray dust, He pulled up reign at the well on the outsets of Ft. Douglas and watered the sorrel gelding and drank also, he took his hat off and dusted off the best he could, he looked into the bucket of fresh water and could see dirt over his entire face, his eyebrows even seemed gray in color from the dust, so he splashed water on his face and removed his bandana and used it to wash off with . . . He wanted a hot bath to clean up, but more than that, he wanted to see Mary Franks . . .

Not to delay it another minute, Wade rode through town to the Roberts home, stepped from the saddle and walked to the door, took a deep breath and tried to swallow, but seemed he had nothing but cotton balls in his mouth . . . He gave three good raps on the door, he could hear footsteps approaching as he tried to manage a smile to his face, he removed his hat abruptly and ran his fingers through his hair . . .

Bill Roberts answered the door, "Well hello Wade, come in, yes, come in, it's been awhile since we last saw you, and you didn't deliver the last load we received, well I figured you had lit out west and wouldn't be seen around here in these parts again" . . .

Wade managed a hand shake, Bill Roberts had the grip of a grizzly, with strong arms and chest, Wade had never feared any man, but for some reason he felt he had some reason to fear this man . . . After all, he had come to call on this mans niece who had been raised as his daughter . . . Silence fell and it felt out of place and awkward for both of them . . .

Bill broke the silence and tension: "I reckon you came to call on Mary, and not to chat with me . . . But I hate to tell you, she's not here . . . Her and Martha took the stage down to Ft. Laramie, they've been gone a few days, and I'm not rightly sure when they will be back, they were planning to take in a few of them shows and an opera of some sort, well to tell you the truth, Mary was feeling down and wanted to get away from town a spell" . . .

"Has she been sick or something"?

"No Wade, not sick, she just needed to get some fresh air for a spell, she'll be alright I reckon when she gets back" . . .

Wade left feeling a little queasy himself . . . He untied the sorrel and stepped into the saddle and rode to the livery stables and bedded him down and gave him some oats, he had been rode hard the last two weeks . . . Wade glanced over and saw Mary's horse still in his stall, a fine looking animal he thought . . . Then walked on down to Charlie Benton's hotel and got a room, took a hot bath and went back to his room and stretched out on the bed, within minutes his eyes were closed . . . He vaguely remembered hearing the late stage roll into town before his eyes fell into the darkness of the night . . .

Mary Franks and her Aunt Martha had been in Ft. Laramie for three days, there had been some traveling shows come through and Martha wanted Mary to experience something new and thought maybe it would help get her mind off Wade leaving, they had took the stage there and had seen all the shows of acting, to dancing, and even a magician, it was an exciting trip, but after a couple of days, Mary was ready to head back to Ft. Douglas, home . . . They had caught the early stage, as there were a couple seats open . . . The stage was an hour late due to a broken hub, they got off the stage in front of Benton's Hotel, retrieved their velvety canvas bags of their belongings and walked down to their house . . . Bill was surprised to see them, as he wasn't expecting them for a few more days . . .

They had been home a good hour when Bill remembered to tell Mary she had a caller: "Oh honey, I almost forgot to tell you, that you had a visitor earlier tonight, a young fellow who looked like he'd been on the trail a bit too long" . . .

"Well who was it uncle Bill"?

"I stood on the porch and watched him go down and bed his horse in and then he walked across the street to Charlie's place, I reckon he's still there" . . .

Martha gave her husband a puzzled look, He simply winked at her, and she smiled knowing all to well who it was, it was almost like a burden had been lifted, but also challenged more burden to enter her mind also, what if he was here today and gone again tomorrow, her little girl would be in more pain than before . . .

Mary had already grabbed up a sash to wrap around her shoulders as the night air was crisp, she was already out the door before Martha could say a word, wrapping the sash over her shoulders as she went down the porch steps . . . She walked as fast as her feet would carry her to Charlie's Hotel, she entered the front door and looked around in the lobby where some of the occupants loitered about, she saw no familiar faces, Charlie Benton was no where in sight, Mary walked to the desk and turned the register around where she looked down the list of names, the last name on the page belonged to Wade Tavner, room number three . . .

She went up the stair way, two steps at a time, and within seconds she was standing at the door of room three, a big brass number 3 hung on the door, she took a deep breath as nerves seemed to well up in her throat . . . She gave a quick three raps on the door, and heard no sound within, she waited a few seconds and knocked again, she could hear the creak of the bed and then feet on the floor, she could hear the footsteps getting closer to the door and then pause momentarily before he opened the door . . .

Wade opened the door cautiously, as he knew not who could be at his door just past dark . . . Standing there was the prettiest woman he'd ever laid eyes on . . .

"Mary, I thought you were in Laramie with your Aunt" . . .

"Well I was, can you not ask a lady into your room"? as she steps past him into the boarding room . . . "Uncle Bill told me you had come by calling on me, did you have business in town that brought you here"?

"No business in town for me, I came only to call on you and for no other reason but to see you" . . . A smile crept out from under his mustache as he could see the twinkle in her eyes as well as he could feel it within his own eyes . . . Looking deep into her eyes made the ride here well worth it . . . Without another word being said, Mary put her arms around behind his neck and pressed her lips to his, his right arm slid around behind her back drawing her close and tight as they had embraced as never before . . .

Wade pushed her back, "You can't be here in my room" . . .

With a puzzled look on her face, "Why can't I"?

"Mary, it wouldn't be proper for you to be here, I am sure folks down the stairs saw you enter my room, and you know how folks like to wag their tongues, you must leave" . . .

"Wade, I don't care what people want to say, I want to be with you" . . .

"Your folks are upright folks in town here, and I will not do anything to disrespect them or cause them undo criticism, I will walk you back to your house and say hello to your Aunt Martha, I am sure she is wondering about you right this minute, I'll meet you for breakfast in the morning . . . OK"?

Mary agreed as Wade reached across to pick up his hat and belted on his colt, then he reached for the door, she slides her hand under his chin and pulls his face towards her and kisses him again . . . Wade was reluctant to open the door, but after a short pause they stepped out into the hallway and walked down the stairs and out the front door . . .

Wade stepped up and held the front door and bode his farewell as Martha opened the door . . .

"Would you like to come in for a spell Mr. Tavner, I could fix a fresh pot of coffee and we have some pie in the pantry"?

"No Ma'am, I couldn't do that, I should be getting back to my room" . . .

Mary grabbed him by his hand, "Nonsense, you can rest later, we just got back from Laramie and we are both starved, so you might as well get in here and keep us company even if you don't want to eat" . . .

"I didn't say I couldn't eat a bite" . . .

It took several minutes before the water was boiling in the pot and by that time the fresh cherry pie was nearly downed and the coffee tasted as good as it smelt . . . Conversation was good with this family, it was a very comfortable home . . .

Wade had walked back to the hotel feeling refreshed, lying down on the bed with the soft down mattress didn't make sleep come easy, for his mind was running rampant with thoughts of Mary Franks . . . He had come here to ask her to go back with him to the valley where he had built his cabin . . . But her home here was so nice and warm, her family was good to her, they loved her it was easy to see . . . How could he step in and take that away from her . . . The night seemed long . . . Sleep was restless . . .

Mary was to meet Wade at Butlers Eatery at seven thirty, and she was there a good fifteen minutes early, dressed in a white blouse with a black riding skirt and black laced up riding boots, her hair was combed down around her shoulders in a neat fashion, she was wearing a black bone necklace fit snugly around her neck in a choker style which accented her hair and facial highlights . . . Wade had come from the livery stable where he had been checking on his horse, and when he stepped up on the boardwalk and got the first glimpse of Mary standing there, his thoughts were that she was the most beautiful woman he had ever seen in his life . . .

Mary took a look at him walking towards her, his leather vest fit neatly around his chest and shoulders, and was tapered to his waist, his shoulders were square and strong, he walked like a man with total confidence of himself, stepping out with a brisk pace, for he knew where he was headed, his arms were strong from hard physical work, he was richly tanned from the sun, he had a manly rugged look about him, with thick dark hair, the creases that framed his eyes from years of riding in the sun gave fine character to his face, his eyes were a bluish green, changing from one color to the other by his mood, eyes that sparkled when he smiled, causing a burning ember that lingers deep in her soul, he smiles freely but can only be seen in his eyes, she thought to herself, this is the most handsome man I ever laid eyes on . . .

They smiled at each other as they walked into Butlers, of course every one in the place knew Mary, and they took a second look when she entered with Wade, arm in arm . . . Wade chose a table in the back of the room, as he always set with his back to the wall and facing the front where he could see anyone who entered the room, and it also gave a view of the street and who was coming and going in town . . . The room was quiet and the tables neatly arranged in a crisscross pattern with a blue denim looking material for table cloths with napkins neatly folded around the silverware . . .

Breakfast was served with slab cut bacon and scrambled eggs with biscuits smothered with sausage gravy . . . It had been along time since Wade had seen eggs for breakfast, eggs were a luxury not feasible riding the trail . . .

After they had both ate their fill, Mary pushed her chair back: "You up for a ride around the country, I'd like to show you some of my favorite spots in the area" . . .

Wade smiled: "You think that ole plug of yours in the stall can make it out of town"?

With a smile of her own: "Should I wait on you to catch up so you won't get lost"?

They left and walked towards the livery, walking past the general store, pausing to tell the Roberts they were going for a ride . . .

Martha stepped to the door quickly: "Do you know where you are going to ride too"?

"I think I will take him out to the falls north of town, Wade hasn't seen them, and I love to ride out there, we will be back before dark Aunt Martha" . . .

"Ma'am, you need not worry about Mary, I will see that no harm comes to her and I will bring her back in one piece" . . .

Martha was worried as all mothers do, Bill walked up as they had left, "She'll be fine ma, they will both be fine, he is a good man I am sure" . . .

The ride out to the falls was a good ride as the weather was nearly perfect, the sun was warm and the breeze light, the falls weren't much of falls for Wade as he had seen falls ten times this size in the mountainous areas, he realized Mary hadn't seen anything other than a days ride from Ft. Douglas, he described the valley to her again in fine detail, Mary had closed her eyes and felt as if she could visualize it to perfection . . .

"Wade, I can't wait to go with you and see it" . . .

"My intentions were to come and ask you to return with me, but Mary, you have such a fine home and family here, I am afraid I can't compete with all of this" . . .

"Wade Tavner, are you asking me to come with you"?

"Mary, I am afraid I" . . . . Mary quickly cut him off, "Now you listen to me Mr. Tavner, you let me decide that decision of whether I want to go or not and that decision has already been made, I want to go so bad I can taste it, yes, I may miss my family, but it is time for me to leave, and I have never met a man before that made me feel like this" . . .

"We need to be heading back then as soon as we can Mary, winter will be settling in before long, or I can go back and get things more ready and come back for you in the spring" . . .

Mary quickly cut him off again, "I will not wait till spring Wade Tavner, we can leave day after tomorrow if you would like" . . .

They rode back to town arriving an hour before dark fell, stopping off at the stables and tending their horses . . . Wade noticed that Mary was good at tending her horse and done a respectful job of it, she had rubbed him down with some soft dry hay fodder she had picked up out of the manger . . .

Telling her Aunt and Uncle would not be an easy task, they would not want to see Mary leave . . . Mary had said she would tell them but Wade insisted he be there too . . . They had planned to leave in two days, that would give time to get things done and say her farewells to her friends she had come to know here in Ft. Douglas . . . Packing would be troublesome, as Mary could only take what could be carried on her horse, but she did not fear the loss of material values . . . She felt she was the luckiest person in the world . . . She was ready to see more of this country . . .

They were packed and ready to leave early, it would be an hour before light shown on the trail ahead, the town was deathly quiet from sound or movement, Aunt Martha was crying, Mary had tears in her eyes too, this had been her home for nearly all her life . . .

Bill Roberts caught Wade outside the door before he entered, he put a grip on Wades arm like a steel trap: "If you don't take care of my little girl, I promise you I will come after you" . . .

Wade didn't take threats from anyone and started to bristle, but then realized, he was taking this mans little girl from him: "I can assure you Bill, I will see no harm come to Mary in any way shape or form, You have my word on that" . . .

Bill released his grip, "Heck I wish I was going with you all, I would love to see more of this country myself" . . .

"Bill, you and Martha are always welcome at our home, we would love to see you come out and set a spell" . . .

The town was quiet as they trotted down through town and headed out into the high plains that stretched out ahead of them, excited as they rode out, it was a new life for them both . . . A life they both were anxious to get started . . . .

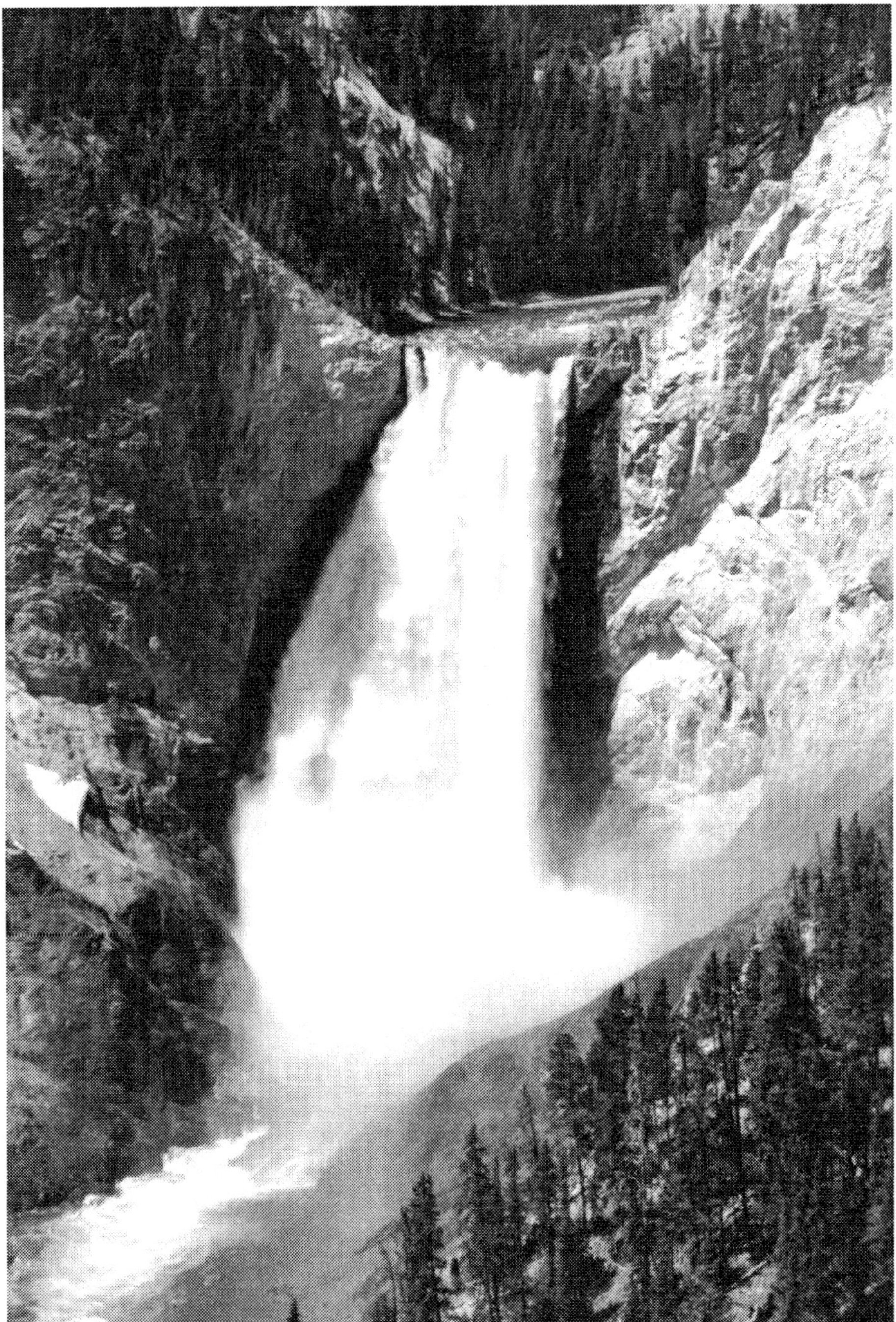

Chapter 5

The morning sun felt good as it warmed their backs as it lifted above the eastern horizon, the prairie lay stretched out ahead of them with an endless sea of prairie grasses waving in the morning breeze, with the scents of the prairie floating endlessly in the air, a hint of sage among the scattered smells of the wild grasses mixed with traces of the dust that lifted from the hooves of the horses . . . Conversation was easy between them as they explored more of each other, little did they know of each others past, and Wade felt just that, the past was the past, he cared not linger on it, but to look to the future, and a bright look it had . . .

Riding at a good pace as the horses were feeling their oats as well this morning, both horses had a competitive edge to them . . . By mid-day they were well out into the open prairies and overtook a huge herd of buffalo, Mary had seen smaller herds in closer to Ft. Douglas, but had never seen the herds like this, they had seen their dust lifting in the horizon for some time and could smell it as the winds were floating from the west, Mary was amazed at their numbers, it was like a sea of animals moving across the prairie and grazing as they went, big and small, there were numerous young ones . . . They skirted to the south of the herd and turned south some as the herd meandered towards the north, Wade knew from traveling through here before that a large lake lay to the north and they were heading towards water . . .

Normally Wade would have traveled west a few more days before turning south if He was wanting to make good time, but He was in a hurry to get back to the cabin as it was getting late in the year, and snows could start falling within the month, but Mary had not seen the mountains and rivers that ran west and north of Denver, Wade had planned to drop down and pick up the western slope and take it out into the high plains of that area . . .

The horses had grown accustomed to each other and traveling with Mary was a pure enjoyment, they had camped several nights out in the open prairies, finding rock outcroppings for what protection they could provide, finding water out here was more difficult late in the year like this too, but Wade had traveled this area before and knew of a few small water holes that were fed by underground springs, and a person with a sharp eye could follow the tracks of antelope and other small animals that also used these water holes, and a rider could pay attention to his horse, for a horse can smell water miles away it seemed . . . Wade would usually shoot a rabbit or ground squirrel for supper and dry roast them on the open fire or sometimes fry them in the skillet . . . Mary never complained of eating wild game . . . Not that there was any choice out here . . .

A week of riding out in the open had tanned Mary's face and arms and it looked good on her . . . The mountains were starting to loom huge to life as they rode closer each day, they seemed large to Mary already, but each day they got bigger and bigger, there was fresh snow on a few of the higher peaks already, but it could snow on some of those peaks in the middle of the summer months, some of the snow there had never melted it appeared . . . The cool breeze was drifting down from the ranges now from where they rode, the smells changed to that of pine and fresh streams that flowed down the ranges out into the flats . . . The water in the streams was clear and cold and tasted good, the air just felt different here, it was crisp and invigorating, it made you want to draw it in deep into your lungs and hold it momentarily before releasing it . . .

They rode around some sharp outcroppings and you could hear the falls well before you could see them, Mary had asked what that roar was, Wade simply told her she would have to wait and see . . . This trail was a little out of the way to their valley, but Wade intentionally wanted to come by these falls for Mary to see, the falls back at Ft. Douglas were no more than five feet, and flat and the water gently rolled over the edge to a small pool below, these falls dropped a good hundred feet or more and were violent crashing into the rocky edges and the ground and stream below creating a foamy lather at the bottom, you couldn't even hear yourself talk standing at the bottom looking up . . . Mary was amazed at the beauty and sound of it as she had never seen anything like this before, she smiled and said "You're right, words cannot do justice to this, a person has to see this for themselves" . . . She breathes in the fresh damp air that floats and drifts into the woods as the falls create a mist in the air, beads of water formed on her cheeks as they stand there . . .

She simply looked at Wade: "I love it Wade, I simply love it" . . .

Wade smiles back with eyes gleaming: "It's only the beginning, it just gets better" . . .

The day has grown late and the sun is low in the sky, they lead their horses a good hundred yards from the falls and set camp close to the lower part of the river, you can still hear the roar of the falls that pounds the rocky cliffs . . .

Morning rolls around with gray skies, Wade is well awake before Mary stirs, he looks at her rolled up in her bedroll and thinks to himself how pretty she is laying there, her eyes crack open as she feels his eyes on her, she smiles back at him through sleepy eyes, he points up to the skies, "We probably should be getting up and on our way, storms may roll in this morning, it could get nasty today . . . Mary pulled the bedroll up and scooted over closer to Wade and pulled it up around his shoulders too, "Let it rain Mr. Tavner, let it rain" . . . Her eyes had a twinkle to them as she scrunched in under his chin . . .

Another hour in the bedrolls was warm and comfy, but after an hour Wade was stirring the coals to bring life to their fire, with a few small twigs placed amongst the coals, there was a blaze within minutes . . . Mary crawls from her bedroll and shakes it out and rolls it up and walks to the fire and warms her hands against the blue and orange flames that dance and flicker into the air . . . Wade was already tending the horses, both had already been rubbed down and pads laying on their backs, saddles were tossed on as Mary went about with finishing up the coffee . . . The sky had turned a little grayer and there was a dampness of drizzle in the air . . .

Wade polished off the rest of his coffee and smothered out the fire and brushed the area of the bedrolls with a broken off pine limb, removing any trace that they had ever been here . . . Mary thought his cautious ways were a little silly, but loved the way that all his ways made her feel safe . . .

"Well Mary Franks, we better be hitting the trail, I think you are going to get a little wet today" . . .

The air had a nip to it this morning as they stepped into the saddles and headed on down the slope towards the western sky . . . Mary pulled out a blue checkered scarf and wrapped around her neck, then tucked it inside her jacket and pulled the collar of her jacket up around her ears with her black felt hat setting on top, she also wore a pair of deer hide riding gloves . . .

Wade couldn't help but take a second look at her, smiling to himself as she didn't catch his look . . . She set her horse as good as any one he'd ever rode with, her horse had settled into the long days of riding as well as Mary had, Wade had noticed her squirming in the saddle some the first few days as riding long hard days takes some getting used too, but she had never complained once of her discomfort, and her horse settled into taking longer strides to keep up with his own mount, her horse rode with a good stride, he looked smooth, his pasterns were off set from his canon bone, Wade always hated to see a horse with straight pasterns as it made for choppy rides most usually . . .

By mid day the drizzle had turned into rain, a rain out of the west, riding straight into it, dipping their heads to keep it out of their faces, hats pulled down low in the front with rain drops dripping from the brims . . .

Wade found a thick patch of spruce trees, heavily needled and grown close together with their outer limbs reaching all the way to the ground . . . He steps from the saddle and pulls the bowie from the back of his gun belt, a thick bladed bowie of a good twelve inches in length, and Wade always kept it sharp . . . He whacked off a few of the limbs on the south east corner of the patch of spruce, it almost looked like a door way, the limbs on the inside had died out from lack of sunshine getting through the thick canopy, they tied the horses close by where there was some good grass and a small spring fed creek for watering . . . Wade kindled a fire and filled both cups of the fresh spring water and boiled up some coffee . . . It was nearly dry inside their makeshift camp . . . The coffee tasted good and was warm going down . . .

"We might as well plan on spending the rest of the day here, we might not find a better shelter than this, and it doesn't look like it's going to clear off today and it's going to get dark early tonight as well" . . .

Mary relaxes the collar from around her ears as the trees have knocked off the damp breeze and the fire had such a warm glow to it, the trees were so thick inside that the smoke barely filtered out through the tops of the trees . . . She heard two shots . . . But minutes later Wade reappeared with the saddles and two gray squirrels . . . "They're a little tough but they got a good taste, they're young ones, them older ones taste to much like pine cones" . . .

Mary had pulled the small skillet from Wade's saddle bag and carved off a hunk of the slab bacon as Wade went about cleaning the squirrels, he took the remains to the small stream and tossed them in to be washed down stream away from their camp and then thoroughly cleaned the remaining pieces of meat, Mary had the skillet hot and ready . . .

Mary rolled them over browning on both sides good: "Some hot biscuits and some gravy would go good with this" . . .

Wade chuckled: "Yeah, and some mashed taters under that gravy and maybe some stewed apples, but it looks like plain ole squirrel for us" . . . But the smell made your mouth water . . .

Dark had set in early with the cloudy skies, Wade took the bottom portion of his bedroll and placed it on stakes that he'd cut that were about two feet tall, and also placed his duster over the back edge making a lean to, then spreading the pine needles thick underneath, then spread Mary's bedroll on top of the pine needles, "Looks like we're sharing a bedroll tonight, it'll be much warmer and as close to dry as we're going to get" . . .

Mary smiled: "Not a problem Wade Tavner, you going to be a gentleman under the same covers"?

"No promises Ma'am" . . .

The fire flickered and crackled into the night as the flames leaped from the wood into the darkness of the night . . . Wade banked it good before turning in for the night as the rain spattered down around their surroundings as they huddled under their makeshift shelter, occasionally the distant lightening would light the night and the rumble of thunder would echo down into the valley floor . . . Mary crowded in close to Wade and thought to herself, she'd never slept so warm and safe . . .

The gray skies of the previous day had opened up to a new fresh looking day as the sun was sending it's warm rays down, They crawled out of the spruce clump and set a fire out in the open this morning as the sun was warm, and it was still shady inside the camp of thick spruces . . . Mary rolled up the bedrolls as Wade kindled the fire back into flames, he had picked up some coals from the fire within with a couple of sticks, so building the fire was quick and easy and there was a blaze within minutes . . . Shortly afterwards was hot coffee to start the day, a quick breakfast and they were ready to head back out on the trail to home . . . The horses had been picketed in fresh grass close to the stream, so they were eager and ready to head out also . . . Wade brushed off their backs with some tough grass he pulled up along side the waters edge, drying their backs off before throwing on the saddles, checking cinches and girths, snugging them loosely around them until just before mounting, letting them settle in . . . Mary could saddle her own horse as good as any man, but was enjoying Wade taking on that responsibility, as she went about doing other things around the camp . . . Just before stepping into the saddle, Wade would always clear any evidence of their camp, Mary had picked this up, so she was well ahead of him . . . They worked together good without even being aware of the fact . . .

They had rode for days with good weather, reaching across the high plains that lay in between the two mountain ranges . . .

Crossing the snowy ranges and down the west slope, they rode through some of the thickest and densest forest yet, the pine needles were thick and spongy underfoot, this was an old forest that had thousands of years of composting of needles and decay, it was near noon and the sun was high in the sky, but you could barely see it from deep in this forest as the canopy above had nearly grown together, only shafts of sunshine filtered down through to the floor of this grand area, an occasional mule deer would snort and quickly disappear into the darkness of trees . . . Riding down they came up into a long valley that stretched out before them, the darkness of trees opened up to a grandeur of tall fresh green grass, grass so dark green it cast a bluish tint as it waved in the afternoon sun, with a stream that roared down off the peaks and rocky cliffs to their west, the stream seemed to rest as it meandered through this valley, switching back and lazily wandering out of sight to the far north end of the valley, grass was nearly to the horses bellies as they rode out into the valley floor, elk were roaming on the eastern side of the valley and bolted up into the tree line when they rode past, with snorts of warning of their visitors, a small band of buffalo wandered about grazing and laying about with full bellies . . .

"Wade, this is beautiful here, I've never seen land so inviting, so breathtaking", as she set her horse looking at the tall granite peaks that lined the west side of the valley, the air was crisp, the sun was warm, only the slightest breeze drifted from the north end of the valley carrying the smell of pine and sage . . . They rode on with Mary taking in every aspect of the day, they had rode to nearly the north end of the valley when Wade turned his horse into a clump of aspens and headed his horse west a bit and towards the granite peaks . . . They were within a hundred feet of the cabin before Mary spotted it, she quickly gave Wade a look of concern . . .

"Welcome home", as he smiled, as he could see a tear well up in her eyes, they stepped from the saddles as Mary walked up on the front porch of the log cabin . . .

"I love it, it's absolutely perfect, I love it, I love it Mr. Wade Tavner", as she throws her arms around his neck and pulls him close and presses her lips to his, he responds as his arm goes naturally around her back and pulls her close to his chest, she flips his hat off and to the ground as she steps up and opens the door and walks inside, eyes gleaming with delight, her excitement bubbles out as never before in her life . . .

The rest of the day flew by as if they had just got here, the sun was softly disappearing behind the granite walls that stood tall behind the cabin, the shadows that cast from the cliffs reached all the way across the valley floor as the elk and mule deer started to wander about, the only noise that could be heard was that of the stream behind the cabin, you could hear it gently babbling and gurgling as it meandered past a few rocks that set next to the bank, the water was deep and cold here and held good trout . . . As night overtook the evening shadows, the occasional hoot of an owl lingered throughout the valley that was answered by a lone coyote yapping his presence into existence, tapering it off with a lone howl into the darkness . . . The thin sliver of the moon was showing itself to the southeast, just barely above the tall thick pines that lined that end of the valley . . .

Mary's heart was so full of joy, she didn't know whether to cry or smile, or maybe both, she looked at Wade, eyes all aglow: "This is picture perfect, this is far better than I ever imagined it even" . . . They were setting on the edge of the front porch as Wade hadn't had time to fashion some chairs for it, but decided that would be one of his next chores to do, as setting here on the porch sipping a cup of fresh coffee watching the sunset with Mary was far beyond his greatest expectations . . . They set silently with not a word of conversation, listening to the sounds of the night, Mary's head had leaned over on Wade's shoulder, her breathing had changed to a more relaxed sound and Wade knew she had fell asleep . . .

The sun had risen in the eastern sky and was casting rays of light that filtered through the aspens and made it's way into the east window of the cabin, Wade jumped to the floor as he hadn't been in bed past sun up in all his life he didn't think . . .

Mary propped herself up on her elbow: "It's alright, the day will wait for us to get there, you in a hurry"?

"We're burning daylight, got things to show you out in the ranch, you've only seen a portion of it, there's two hidden valleys here, one back behind the cabin in those tall granite cliffs, it's a thousand feet up and levels off to a wide open meadow with a small falls at the back of it, there's only one trail up to it, but I think we can get the cattle up to it for summer grazing" . . .

"Ok, ok", as Mary flips the blanket back from the bed and steps out onto a buffalo hide rug placed at the edge of the bed and pulls on one of Wades shirts and her riding pants and laces up her boots . . .

Wade looks at her standing there wearing his faded denim shirt and catches himself thinking to himself, "what's the hurry" . . .

It's mid morning by the time they get out and saddled up, the horses feeling fresh and frisky as they seem to know they are home too . . . Wade takes her up to the hidden valley above, stashed away in those granite walls, riding out to the edge of it gives a man a view of the entire valley floor, the edge falls to nearly a straight drop to the bottom, the cabin is in view and the thin thread of smoke drifts effortlessly above the stone flue, lifting nearly straight up as the breeze is non existent . . .

The day was gone before they seemed to even get started . . . Tomorrow would be a new day . . .

"I need to start a shelter for the horses and a make a place for the tack and store up some loose hay, you never know what winter will bring out here" . . . Mary was eager to help . . .

They spent the next week cutting poles and building stables. They made it large enough to accommodate a loft to which they filled with long stem native grass . . . They set up poles for a corral with a swinging gate, hanging on leather hinges of some of the buffalo hide Wade had tanned earlier, the horses could now be turned out into the corral . . . A makeshift trough was made by hollowing out a log and leaving the ends intact, Wade rubbed it down with buffalo fat, repeating the process till it wouldn't take up any more, making it water tight, he then notched it into two small logs setting on the ground to keep it from being knocked over . . .

The days were filled with hard work for them both, but it felt good at the end of the day to be tired from what a man's hands could do and look back at the end of the day and feel good about what you had accomplished . . .

They added another room on the side of the stables for their tack and supplies . . . Then they found a spot in the side of the mountain where they could dig into it making a food cache . . . Digging back a good ten feet or more, shoring it up with log poles, it was mostly rock on the top side, making a log frame entrance, it looked like the opening of a mine shaft, then Wade cut poles and made a door that mounted firmly on the frame opening, it would stay cool in it during the summer and it was deep enough that it wouldn't freeze inside it during the winter . . . They fashioned shelves against the back wall to stack things on, with a pole across one side to hang meat on . . . Eager to try it out, they went out and shot a nice young mule deer and quartered him up and hung him to cure . . .

The aspens had turned a golden yellow on the western slopes of their surroundings as winter approached, Wade decided they needed to take a couple days and head over to Silver Creek Springs and pack up on supplies for the winter . . . He warned Mary of what a mining boom town was like, she had never seen a boom town, she had heard stories of such places, but Wade didn't want her to expect a town anything like Ft. Douglas . . . Rising early the next morning, Wade stepped out to the porch and evaluated the western sky, it all looked clear with a promise of a good day, although the air was cold this morning, but if it had looked like a storm brewing, they would have stayed home and gone another time . . . Saddled up they headed out the north end of their valley, horses were eager to be out and set a good pace, each with a competitive spirit, after a couple hours of riding briskly, they pulled up to let the horses blow, then the pace seemed to relax a bit as the horses grew into the days ride ahead . . .

Riding into Silver Creek Springs late afternoon, the place had taken a drastic change since the last time Wade had been here, most of the canvas tents that were set up for business had been replaced with false front wood framed buildings, the place was a buzz with activity, folks on the street riding horses, pulling donkeys, buckboards, horses of all sizes and shape it seemed . . . There were two general stores, a hotel at one end of the street, four or five supposedly lawyer land offices, and five saloons . . . Mary was all eyes taking in all the activity of the place, but one thing she had noticed, there were probably thirty men to every woman she saw . . . The men were mostly miner types, dirty from their diggings, and the women didn't look like the home body type . . . Wade started to get ruffled a bit as the hair stood on the back of his neck as he noticed every man in town was looking at Mary, but tried to push the thought off, after all, she was the prettiest woman any of these men had ever seen, heck, she was the prettiest thing He had ever seen . . . The town had grown a little rougher though he could tell, this type of town didn't draw family folks, the men here were looking to get rich quick, and to some of them, it didn't matter how they did it and to who's expense . . . The carpetbaggers had moved in too . . . Those law offices were mostly likely shysters too . . . He knew he wouldn't trust his neck to any of the lot . . .

They rode down to the general store and stepped inside, Mary was taking it in as she knew this business to perfection . . . She smiled at Wade as she saw him watching her inventory the store . . . Wade too, had already sized up where things were at, who was standing where, who was behind the counter . . . Mary started filling the list of goods they had came to buy, she was amazed at the place, it was nothing compared to her Uncle's store, it had more digging tools and such as picks and spades and grubbing hoes, it was interesting to say the least, she was nearly done when a young fellow wearing a long black oil tanned duster stepped into the store, Wade instantly pegged him as trouble, he wore a colt tied low on his leg, his eyes were on Mary, that was reason enough for Wade to not like him already, the man stepped across the room towards Mary and removed his hat and asked her if he could help in any way . . .

Mary gave him one short look: "No thanks, we've got all we need", and looked towards Wade who had just stepped up beside her as she set her goods on the counter . . . He introduced himself as Billy Slade, the name meant nothing to Wade, he had not heard it before and didn't care, but stuck out his hand: "Nice to meet you Billy Slade, guess we'll settle up here and be on our way" . . .

They loaded up their stuff into four burlap bags that could be thrown over the back of the saddles and started for the door . . .

Billy Slade stepped in Wades path . . . . Stopping him, with contempt in his eyes: "I didn't get your name or the pretty lady here" . . .

Wade quickly looked the man straight in the eyes, Wades eyes had instantly turned a cold gray, a look he hadn't felt in some time, he could feel the anger boil up within himself, there was no fear within him, instinctively he had already slipped the bag to his left hand, and brushed his coat back leaving his own colt in view and easy access, he had been here before . . .

Mary quickly stepped up between them and stuck out her hand: "We're sorry, my name is Mary and this here is Wade, it's good to meet you, did you say your name was Billy? Wade, are you ready, as we need to be on our way" . . .

Wade gave the man a look of death as he stepped past him, stepping out into the street and tying the bags of goods on the horses, stepping into the saddles, Wade reined the horse around and headed out the west side of town, Mary looking at him with puzzlement as to why they were heading the wrong direction, but she knew to trust him with her life . . .

They rode west a good stretch out of town then cut a path south of town and stayed well into the trees . . .

"What is it Wade, did you know that man"?

"No, I didn't know the man, never heard his name before either, I just know the type, and he thought you were going to be the prize" . . .

Mary laughs" "Well that's not going to happen" . . .

Wade tried a smile as he took that as a compliment, "But you don't understand Mary, the man was looking for trouble, he is trouble" . . .

They spent the night camped along a small stream south of Silver Creek Springs with a minimal amount of fire, and the fire was built back under a spruce, thick of needles, with only the driest of wood, what little bit of smoke was made, quickly disappeared into the spruce . . . Wade had checked his colt as he always did, but this time it was more than just a simple routine, and as they sacked in for the night, he lay the Winchester close to Mary's side . . . Sleep was of little use for Wade as he listened to every sound of the night air . . . Mary slept like a log as she lay cuddled up beside Wade . . .

Wade was more than eager to be back on the trail as soon as the sun crept into existence, he pushed the horses harder than normal, but was a good feeling when they rounded the north end of the rocky outcroppings and headed into their valley, the cabin was refreshing as the mountain breeze with the sound of the stream floating effortless in the wind . . . It was truly good to be home . . . A home it was . . . .

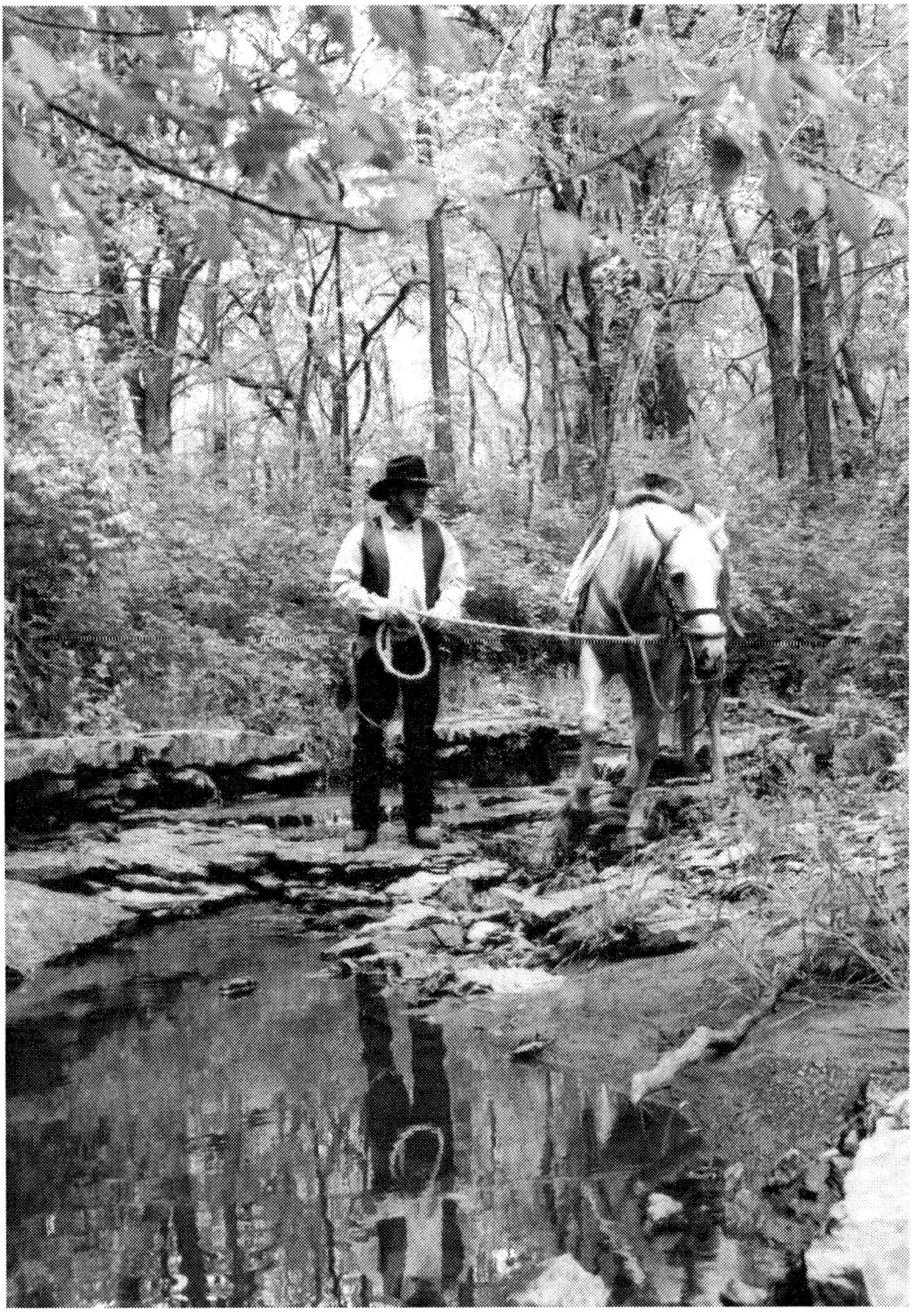

Chapter 6

The breeze was flickering in what was left of the golden aspen leaves, a hint of winter was in the air, as Wade lifted the axe to split another log for firewood, the breeze had a bite to it, it stung his ears as he went about his chores of stacking up ricks of chord wood . . . Mary stepped out with a fresh cup of coffee, two cups, as they strolled back to the front porch and set in the chairs that Wade had made from aspen limbs, using strips of tanned leather woven together for the seat, with a spindle back and arm rests . . . They had cut poles and limbs and such and had them drying in the loft of the barn, Wade would use those later, making furniture for inside the cabin during winter months . . . He had bought a crosscut saw so he could saw slabs off bigger logs for tabletops and such . . .

The days were filled with work for preparation of the oncoming of winter and snows, Wade didn't know how much snow would fall in the valley, he had never been here during the winter months, but he wanted to be well prepared for the worst . . . He had witnessed too well, what devastations could occur if a man wasn't prepared for it . . . The days were much shorter now as the sun would drop below the granite walls before five o'clock, and the morning shadows stayed till nearly seven thirty or so, the sun was well into the southern skies, the day time temperatures were staying colder each day, ice would be formed on the water bucket setting on the porch each morning . . .

The sun had disappeared early today as the sky turned a dark gray, stepping from the porch and studying the western sky just as the last bit of daylight lit their valley . . .

"Mary Franks, I think we're going to get our first real snow tonight, I probably ought to bring in some extra wood and stack some under the porch roof too" . . .

Mary seemed of little concern of the snow: "You might just have to stay inside with me tomorrow, I can show you how to cook and you could help me stitch some on that quilt and well" . . .

Wade cut her off as he laughs: "Ain't nobody going to teach me how to cook, I've been feeding myself since I was a pup, way before you came along, and I don't need no fancy quilt to keep me warm" although he thought it was a fine looking quilt, with all the blues and whites placed strategically around in a star pattern, he reaches up and grabs her by the hand and pulls her off the porch and into his arms, catching her off guard . . . Smiling: "You got anything else to teach me"?

Mary started to step past him, but only put her left leg behind his right leg and gave a quick shove to his shoulders, Wade stammered backwards but couldn't stay on his feet as he fell to his back with Mary landing on top of him: "I'll teach you a thing or two mister, I'll teach you" . . .

Wade partially startled and felt as clumsy as a young colt laying there flat on his back, "Is that the best you got", as he quickly wrapped both arms around her and pinned both her arms next to her body and rolled over to where she was on the bottom, pine needles hanging in her hair from the ground . . .

"You don't scare me Mr. Wade Tavner" . . . Darkness fell into their valley as they rolled around like a couple of bear cubs frolicking about, enjoying the companionship of each other . . . The night air seemed to loose it's chilling feeling . . .

Wade rose early, the sky still seemed dark and gray, but there was a lightness in the cabin that was different, he stoked a flame into the fire and put on a couple more sticks as the fire had died down during the night, he stepped to the front door and opened it to see the entire valley floor was covered with snow, the surrounding peaks were totally covered and you could see the wind swirling it around from peak to peak, he looked over to Mary, still laying in bed and held the door open so she could see, she simply pulled the covers up over her head and snuggled deeper into the warmth of the bed . . .

Wade pulled on his boots and his warmest coat and set his hat, then stepped out to tend the horses . . . It was a wet snow, it had stuck to everything, the trees were covered with the new snow, it was a good six inches or better . . . The valley was beautiful . . .

Mary had crawled from the warm covers to stand by the now blazing fire, which glowed out into the cabin with brightness and warmth, the cabin was solid built and tight . . . Mary opened the front door to peak out at the new surroundings and to see what Wade was doing, just as she stuck her head around the door frame, "SPLAT", a snowball landed square in the middle of the door and splattered fresh snow on her . . . The door slammed shut as Wade could hear her mumble inside: "You'll pay for that Mr. Tavner, trust me, you'll pay" . . . Wade smiles to himself as he goes about the rest of the chores of feeding the horses and breaking the ice in the trough and carrying fresh water for them . . . The horses seemed eager to get out this morning, the chill in air and the fresh snow had made them feel frisky . . .

Wade came in for breakfast and proposed a ride out into the valley this morning . . . Mary was all for it . . .

He made sure their backs were clean and free of any snow and saddle blankets were thrown on, letting them warm up, then the saddles, he warmed the bits in his hands before putting on the headstalls . . . Wade heard the cabin door shut, but before he could turn around to see Mary dressed in her warmest gear, a wet snowball hit him square in the back sending snow up against his hat which fell down inside his coat collar, followed by a giggle . . . He just shook his head . . . He knew he had it coming, he had met his match . . .

They rode down towards the south end of the valley, where the stream fell from the higher peaks, the trees were iced up from the mist, the sun had broken through the gray skies, creating one beautiful sight, looking back up the valley, framed by peaks on both sides . . . The mountains change contrasts during the seasons . . . During the summer months the greenness of the pines and aspens and undergrowth all seem to grow together and the patches of snow in the high peaks stand out and catch your eye . . . Then fall arrives and the aspens stand out against the sea of green of the pines with spots of yellow and orange and gold, contrasting each other . . . Now the ground is white, the pines stand alone in color, they seem greener now than before, the aspens are bare and their white trunks blend in against the snow as if they don't even exist . . . There's enough movement in the water in the stream that it stays open and clear, it seems to have changed colors too, it seems darker contrasted against the white background of the snow . . .

Riding along the eastern portion of the valley, they jump several groups of elk, mostly cows and younger ones, the bigger bulls have moved away from the main herd and are gathered together in groups of bachelor bulls higher up on the slope . . . Half the day is gone by the time they ride back to the cabin, coming in from the north end of the valley is a herd of buffalo, grazing as they move along . . . Wade tried counting them as they moved past, but lost track, but there were several hundred . . . Thinking to himself, if buffalo can winter here, so can cattle . . .

The winter had come and gone with days of both more snow and days of sunshine too, some snow melted days after it fell, in some areas it had lasted all winter, the high meadow above their cabin had stayed snowed in all winter, but the valley floor where their cabin set had never been covered so much where the buffalo couldn't find grass beneath it . . .

Wade was getting eager to set out to buy cattle for their range this next summer . . . They would build a pole line fence across the north end to contain them in the valley, the rest of the canyon was pretty much closed off, a man and a good horse could ride out the south end alright, but cattle weren't that adventurous, they would stay where there was grass and water, and there was plenty of that in the three valleys within this range of peaks . . . Wade smiled to himself thinking that would be a good name for their ranch . . . Three Valleys Ranch, that had a good sound to it . . . Wade ran it past Mary, and she agreed, Three Valleys Ranch it was . . .

Chapter 7

    The winter had played it's hand, and now spring was taking back over, the days grew longer each day, the aspens were starting to bud out, as new life began to form right in front of your own eyes, purple flowers were sprouting on the slopes that received full sunlight, that warmed the ground and had melted away what was left of the snow, everything around you seemed refreshed, coming out of the dormancy of winter . . .

    Supplies were running low as they hadn't been to town in nearly five months, there was an endless supply of meat with the elk and buffalo, but a man couldn't live on meat alone . . . A trip into Silver Creek Springs was on the agenda of things that had to be done . . . They waited for a good clearing spell in the weather and saddled up and headed out the north end of the valley for town, a good twenty miles away, a hard days ride in this country this time of year, the streams would be bank full with all the snow melt and the low lying areas would be marshy, you had to ride the rocky slopes as much as possible . . .

    It was a marvelous day of sunshine and warm weather, every animal that inhabited the area seemed to be out and about early this morning, the ride was good as the horses were eager to be out as well, they'd been stalled up most of the winter with few trips farther than what lay inside Three Valleys Ranch . . . Wade would stop a little more frequently as the horses would need to stop and blow a bit, as he would stroke his big sorrel on the neck, "What's a matter big fella, you get soft laying around all winter burning hay, might have to work you back into shape" . . .

    The sun was setting low when they rode into Silver Creek Springs, it was half past six . . . Wade had already figured they'd have to spend the night in town and get supplies first thing in the morning and head back . . .

Amazed at how the town had really grown even through the winter months with lumber built businesses along both sides of the street now, the street was muddy from the melting of snow and a few spring rains . . . Riding into town from the east, just as they got to the edge of town, Wade noticed a small group of people gathered around just passed the third store front, there was small alley way that led to the back of the buildings, one of the saloons was next to it . . . As they rode up even with the commotion, Wade saw a man lying on the ground, another man just kicked him in the ribs, the folks in town mostly were trying to ignore that anything was going on, Wade could not stand for an injustice to anyone . . . He steps down from his horse, instinctively flips the tie down off the hammer of his colt and steps in to see what is going on . . . The man on the ground had blood coming from behind his left ear and he was holding his ribs, a third man from the other side hollers to him as he kicks him again . . .

Wades blood started flowing through his veins at a higher rate as he steps in: "This man do you wrong in a way he deserved this"?

The man holding a bottle of whiskey turns around and gives him a look of pure defiance, that someone would even question his authority of whatever he wanted to do . . . A dirty sarcastic smile writhes across his face, a face Wade had seen before . . .

There were four men in on the beating you could tell, the man on the other side hollers across to Wade: "He's just an old mex, aint' that enough reason" . . .

Wade took another step towards them: "I don't care if it's a dog, you ain't going to beat him like that, not if he don't have it coming . . .

The man with the bottle was obviously the man leading the other three, he steps to his left a bit and brings Wade in towards the middle of them: "Maybe you would like to take the mex's place, maybe you got a whooping due yourself" . . .

Wade took a step closer, there was no backing down in him, if the man was bluffing, Wade just called his hand: "You touch him again and you will have to deal with me" . . . As his eyes turned a cold gray and it was as though he could see right through the man . . .

The third man laughed out loud: "Mister, you don't know who that is do ya? That there is Billy Slade, Billy Slade I tell ya" . . .

"Is that supposed to mean something"?

You could see the anger start to boil in Billy Slade, this man had rode into his town and questioned his authority, the name Billy Slade meant nothing to him, this angered him even more, but he had not seen a man that showed no sign of fear as this, there were four of them, and only one man stood so tall . . . Their eyes had been totally on Wade, they had seen Mary step from the saddle and went to the man on the ground, she was holding a bandana on the back of his head, they never noticed that when she slid off her horse that she had pulled the Winchester out of Wades saddle, and going to the man on the ground she laid it beside him, close, next to his body . . .

Billy Slade took a step farther out into the street, pulling his duster back away from his sidearm: "I started this and I plan to finish it when I'm done, you ain't going to stop me", and he leaned to his left and spit on the old man lying on the ground and then pitched the bottle to one of his cohorts standing on the steps of the boardwalk, the other two looked worried, they were fine with this as long as no one took a stand against them, but now the fun was gone, and they stepped a few feet to the side, they had no thoughts of someone dying or getting shot, and this man had no fear of them, maybe they would get shot too, the possibilities of that didn't sound like so much fun . . . You could see, the two wanted nothing of it now . . .

Mary had a desperate look on her face, she had vaguely heard stories and rumors of Wade and his gun, but had never seen anything taking place like this, she was worried for him to say the least, they had simply come for supplies and all this transpired in minutes of getting into town . . .

Billy Slade knew he had the edge, or he might not have been so brave, but he couldn't back down now either, as people in the town had gathered about . . .

Billy only thought he had the edge, he knew nothing of the man standing in front of him . . . Billy had never actually had to kill anyone, he had always gotten by with his bullying folks around, no one had ever crossed him like this . . .

Wade knew the tricks of what was transpiring, Wade knew all to well that every gunfighter is looking for the slightest of advantages, you can even beat some one faster than you if you have that one little advantage . . . The whiskey bottle was the trick Billy thought he had, for his partner was going to drop it when he touched his hand to his hat, that was the signal for him to drop the bottle on the steps, knowing that Wade would look quickly to see what the noise was and Billy would go for his gun at that moment . . . This was not something these two had invented, Wade had learned that trick many years ago, and now it would be to his advantage . . .

Wade looked him cold in the face, not wavering, no sign of sweat, eyes cold and calculating: "You can walk away, no one will get hurt" . . .

Billy scoffs at the proposal, a jittery smile creeps across his face as he lifts his hand to his hat, his partner drops the bottle to the steps . . .

Wade instinctively jerks his head in that direction, but little did they know, Wades gun was already coming to his hand the second before he turned his head, the colt came out with ease, and leveled off at Billy Slade's chest, Billy's gun hadn't quite cleared leather when he saw smoke billow from the end of Wades colt, the smile left his face and his eyes showed nothing but fear in them, his own gun went off and plowed into the ground inches from his own feet, he fell face down in the mud of the street . . .

Wade quickly turned to the man standing on the steps: "Your turn, you want some of this action"?

Wade heard the distinct sound of a rifle being levered to action, he looked to his right and Mary was standing there holding the Winchester at the two at the other end, the man had his gun hand down low, he never dreamed that he would even need to use it, he had figured his friend Billy a sure thing, the other two took off at a run to the livery stables and within minutes you could hear the pounding of hooves leaving town . . .

Wade holstered his gun: "Looks even now, just you and me" . . .

"Well not really, if he shoots you, he'll have to shoot me and that woman over there too it looks like" . . . came a voice from behind Wade, a voice he knew well, the voice belonged to Roger Mcnall . . .

The man pulls his hand away from his gun, beads of sweat quickly forming on his forehead: "I got no quarrel with any of you" . . .

"Get your friend there out of the street and get out of town then, if we run into each other again, it might not end so friendly for you" . . .

He got a couple of the other town folks to help him remove Billy's body from the street as they drag him over to the undertakers wood framed building . . .

Roger Mcnall stepped up: "Well well . . . I came to town wondering if I could find you anywhere abouts, this morning it seemed that no one here ever heard of Wade Tavner, until now that is, I'll be willing to bet you by the end of the day, they will all know who Wade Tavner is" . . .

Wade shook his hand: "Good to see you, what brings you out this far"?

"Just had a load coming this way and thought I needed to get out of Denver for a bit, and thought maybe I'd run into you up here somewhere, see if you was ready to come back to work for me", he looks toward Mary standing there still holding the rifle, "but I can see that ain't likely, and I would add, I don't blame you a bit" . . .

"Roger, how long you hanging around this part of the country"?

"Just a day or so, got work to do you know, thought I'd visit around town here and maybe pick up some more work, got a few more drivers since you left, got to keep work for em all" . . .

"You might as well swing out to the ranch, I'll draw you a map out to it, in fact, if your hauling empty going back, I could use a load of things from town myself" . . .

"Sounds like an invitation, I was hoping to see this valley you've been dreaming of for the last couple years, You going to introduce me to this fine looking woman" . . .

Mary had went back to doctoring the old man laying in the mud, she had about got the bleeding stopped, he was setting up, with his back resting against the boardwalk . . . You could tell he was a Spaniard, he had probably been in this country longer than any of us . . . He looked to be a good seventy years of age, his clothing showed that he had come from Spanish royalty at some point in his life . . . He wasn't a mex, he was Spanish . . . His trousers were of leather and they had silver rowels down the outer seam, a couple were missing, a tapered cut leather vest that didn't quite fit so neatly anymore, but you could tell he was accustomed to fine clothing . . . There was no doctor in town, Wade and Mary tended him the best they could, no one else in town offered any help . . .

Mary wanted to get some bandages from the general store, so they told the older gent to stay put and they'd be right back . . . Roger had to go across the street and said he would catch up with them later . . . They returned in just a few minutes, but the old fellow was gone, and nowhere in sight . . . They looked behind the stores and in the stables, but he was gone . . .

They had made arrangements to meet Roger for dinner at the local dining hall at seven thirty, they planned to get a room at the hotel and get their supplies in the morning . . .

Supper was venison, there wasn't nothing in the place with beef in it, a good sign to a man getting ready to raise beef in the area . . . Conversation with an old friend was good . . .

The room at the hotel was sufficient, but neither of them thought it beat their own abode with the moss filled mattress . . . It was a restless sleep for Wade, as the sounds of the nightlife in town lingered well into the darkness of night . . .

They had met Roger for breakfast also, bacon and eggs with biscuits and sausage gravy, it tasted as good as it smelt . . . Roger was going to haul supplies out to the ranch for them, so they got more things than they could have otherwise . . . Wade even got enough lumber bought to put a wood floor in the cabin . . .

They walked up to the general store, and there set a young boy, around ten I'd a guessed, he had himself a passel of pups, trying to sell them for two bits apiece, cute dogs, and Wade reached down to pet one of them . . . Wade walked in to the store, but Mary wasn't beside him, he looked back and she was still standing at the door, holding one of them little golden colored pups, he had cuddled himself up under her chin, Wade wasn't sure which one, the pup or Mary, had the saddest looking eyes . . .

Wade shook his head no: "We sure don't need no dog around the place" . . .

"But Wade, look at him, isn't he the cutest thing you ever saw" . . .

"He'll grow out of it, look at the size of those feet, he'll be a big dog Mary" . . .

"I have always wanted my own dog, please" . . .

Like I said, those were the saddest eyes I ever did see, I just shot and killed a man last night, and now just got whipped by pretty blue eyes . . . "Well I'm not carrying him back, he's your dog, remember that" . . .

It was amazing how fast those blue eyes went from sad to gleaming, "You won't have to worry about him, he will be just fine with me, I'll take good care of him" . . .

Chapter 8

Roger had spent a couple of days at the ranch, we had unloaded the supplies and he even helped me lay the floor in the cabin . . . The wood plank floor sure made a difference . . . Roger had sure enjoyed the stay as well as we enjoyed the company . . .

Roger was harnessed up and ready to roll out: "Wade, you've got it, I wouldn't trade a million dollars for what you have here, this is one of the prettiest valleys I've ever laid my eyes on, and a woman to match . . .

The golden colored pup had been dubbed with the name of Roscoe, well that was what Mary had named him, Wade just called him "dog" . . .

He whined the first few nights, Mary had been up and pampered him half the night . . . "Mary, he ain't getting in bed with us now, don't even think that, not even for a minute" . . . Wade woke up with a ball of yellow fur nuzzled next to his ear . . .

"Dang dog, I said he wasn't sleeping on the bed" . . . Roscoe's tail was wagging and Mary was smiling ear to ear and her eyes had that gleam of a laugh in them . . . Wade went out to tend the horses and the rest of the morning chores, Roscoe leaped from the bed and followed him to the barn . . . Wade caught himself talking to the dog, and Roscoe would set and look at him with his head cocked sideways, occasionally Wade would reach down and rub his head between his ears . . . Roscoe learned quickly that horses would kick . . . Wade would occasionally toss a stick out in the grass and Roscoe would quickly run and bring it back to Wade and drop it at his feet . . .

They had been back from town five days, it was early morning, the sun wasn't breaking the horizon yet, Roscoe was setting on the edge of the bed growling towards the front door of the cabin, Wade lay there wide awake listening to the sounds of the morning, a few birds chirped their morning echoes from behind the cabin, but all was silent out front, then Wade heard a sound from towards the barn, not a sound common to what the horses would have made, then he heard the creak of the barn door where the tack and supplies were kept . . . Wade was quickly to his feet, as well as Mary, he handed her the Winchester and took the colt and slipped out the back door, Mary had cracked open the window on that side facing the barn, peering out into the dusk of the morning, Wade had moved like a ghost across the yard to the side of the barn, opening the tack door easily and peering inside, nothing, but Wade saw a track of a foot print just inside the doorway in the soft dirt, the tracks stepped back out and then went around to the front, Wade quickly glanced at the horses, they were standing eating on some grass hay, not seeming to be alarmed of anything or anyone, He slipped around to the front door of the barn, the outside latch was off, he knew he had shut it last night . . . Swinging the door open, he stepped inside and to the right into the shadows of darkness, standing motionless and letting his eyes adjust to the dark . . . Wade heard movement above in the loose hay in the loft, slipping across the barn floor to the ladder and quietly climbed to the top, lying there in the hay lay the old Spaniard . . . He was asleep, tired from his travel here, he must have walked the whole way . . . Wade slipped back out as quietly as he came in, walking back to the cabin, Mary quickly stepped out on the porch, still holding the Winchester with Roscoe close beside her, with the hair standing on the back of his neck . . .

Mary looking into his face: "What was it"?

"Well it seems we have company" . . .

Mary's eyebrow quirks down a bit: "And who or what is it"?

"The old Spanish fellow from Silver Creek Springs" . . .

"You going to make him stay in the barn"?

"Mary, he's asleep, he didn't even know I was there, he looked worn out, we'll let him sleep and when he gets up we'll figure it out, who knows, he may be gone as silently as he showed up" . . .

It was late afternoon when the old Spaniard rose from his sleep, Wade was setting a post out on the north side of the barn, when he stepped around and offered to help Wade dig the hole . . . Wade handed him the jobbers, he rolled his sleeves and went to it, smiling occasionally at Wade, when the hole was a good two feet deep, Wade stopped him, "Good enough" and walked to the bucket of fresh water with the dipper, Wade tilted the dipper and let it fill and handed it to the ole fella . . . He motioned for Wade to drink first, so Wade drank his fill then refilled the dipper and handed it back, the old Spaniard drank deep, as a horse that just traveled across the desert . . . "We dig again"?

Wade shook his head no: "You must be hungry" . . . Mary was already ahead of them as she was walking across the yard towards them, holding a tin plate filled with a leftover hunk of buffalo steak with a biscuit lying next to it with some beans smothered across the plate on the other side . . .

His eyes took on a gleam that hadn't been seen in some time, he quickly took the plate and headed for the barn . . . Wade grabbed his arm: "Come set on the porch with us, we can all share some coffee as well" . . . The Spaniard shook his head that he should go to the barn to eat, but Wades grip didn't release his arm until he turned and walked to the cabin with them . . .

The ole Spaniard ate like he hadn't seen food in some time, he quickly cleaned the plate and using the remains of the biscuit sopped up anything that was left, the plate was as clean as if it had been washed . . . His English was broken, but spoke well enough to communicate alright . . .

Wade looked at him: "You headed somewhere" . . .

"You save life, me stay here, work for you, repay my debt" . . .

Wade smiled: "You owe me nothing sir, you have no debt to repay, maybe you would have done the same for me one day" . . .

They sat and talked most of the afternoon, he had a fine background, his ancestors from long ago had come to the new world with Cortez, they had brought horses and cattle up from Mexico, they had raised some of the finest horses . . . They had fought against the Apaches . . . He had been driven from his home . . . As far as he knew, he had no family left . . . He talked of the great horses he once owned . . . He had a long drawn out fancy name, but told us we could call him Ramos . . . He didn't seem eager to leave, in fact he was looking for a place to call home . . .

Wade and Mary discussed the situation, they couldn't tell him to leave, they couldn't just throw him out, maybe he would leave on his own in a week or two . . .

Ramos had been a good help on the ranch, corrals were added as well as a rail fence at the north end of the valley, closing it in from the high plains that reached to the north from there . . .

Ramos inquired of Wade: "Where will you buy your cattle now that you are ready for them"?

"I reckon we will have to go back east over the passes and south, there are some ranches down that way where we can buy stock" . . .

"Señor, I know where there are cattle running loose a few days south of here, it is rough country, they are wild cattle, mostly longhorns, brought up from Mexico, no one owns them, the Indians ran them off from the early Spanish settlers, there are a few hundred I am sure" . . .

The idea was very intriguing, but rounding up wild cattle and driving them back to here with just the three of us, and one being an old man, who had no horse . . . The idea grew on Wade the more he thought of it, but first he needed another horse, and saddle . . . Wade told Ramos they would try it, he would ride to town and see if he could find a good horse and a saddle for Ramos, he invited Ramos to go along, but Ramos wanted nothing to do with Silver Creek Springs: "There are no good people in that town, they all want to get rich, they care for nothing but money" . . . But he told Wade to not buy him a saddle, just get him a decent horse, then he dug in his vest pocket and pulled out a twenty dollar gold coin, it was all the money he had to his name, but insisted he need not a saddle, bring him a horse and he would show them . . .

Wade saddled up early the next morning, Mary was staying at the ranch with Roscoe and Ramos as Wade intended to make the ride in short time, he left the Winchester with Mary and headed out into the high plains before the sun rose, Mary had fixed him a bag of biscuits and jerky which he stashed in the saddle bags . . . The sorrel was feeling good under the saddle as Wade set him to a strong pace, they could hear Mary's horse whinnying to them long after they left . . . The ride felt good to Wade, it felt good to be out and covering ground like this, but thought to himself, he sure wouldn't go back to this for an everyday lifestyle now . . .

Riding into town mid afternoon, he went straight to the livery, they had seven horses in the corral out back, none of them really anything to brag about, a couple were too old, two had bad feet, one had a cut on his withers . . . You got anything else, or anyone else around got a good horse for sale . . . The hostler mentioned one in the stalls: "He's a young horse, not broke good and the man wants too much money for him" . . .

"Let's see him, how much does he have to have for him"?

Jim Wilson was the owner of the Livery Stables, a middle aged man, who didn't carry a gun, a honest looking man to Wade, not normal for a horse trader, a man with strong arms and back, but a pleasant nature to him, and a good handler of horses . . .

"He belongs to the new banker down the street, he's asking twenty five dollars for the animal, he brought him out here from back east, but he can't ride the beast", the ole hostler laughs a little, "but he ain't a horse man either, I think the horse is a good animal, I saw the banker fella hitting him for not doing what he wanted, hell that just made things worse, then the man got off without getting him out of the stall, that horse learned real good didn't he", as he chuckled more . . . And forced a smile across Wades face also . . .

Wade looked him over real good, he was a fine animal for sure, good confirmation, good solid feet, "You think this banker fella would take twenty dollars for him"?

"I wouldn't say sir, you'd have to ask him, but he's a losing money on him, paying me to feed and stall him every month and he can't even ride him" . . .

Wade strolled down to the bank and stepped in, a few customers were standing about, but quickly done their business and left when Wade walked in . . . He looked about and found the manager setting behind a small wooden desk back behind the counter with all the bars set forth, he asked to speak to the man, the man had a weasel type face, kind of pinched in towards his nose, a little mustache cut short and trimmed tight, beady eyes to boot . . . He acted startled that Wade wanted to speak to him, Wade walked around the corner of the counter and through the little short swinging door, the man had his right hand in his lap, Wade figured there was a gun under the desk, which he figured wasn't a bad idea for a banking man . . .

Wade walked right up to him briskly, "You the man who owns the horse down at the livery"?

"Why yes I am", he looked relieved that was what Wade wanted, "He's a fine animal too I might add" . . .

"He ain't broke and it appears that he needs some work, the man down there says your wanting twenty five dollars for him, if he was good and broke maybe, but not like that, you ain't going to get that much for him around here, these miners don't even like horses, I'll give you eighteen for him, as is" . . .

The banker tried to smile a bit, "I can keep him for that" . . .

"I wouldn't know why, you can't ride him and never will", Wade reached into his pocket and pulled out the twenty dollar gold coin and flipped it to him, "Even trade, it's more than you'll get from anyone else here abouts" . . . Wade knew that a banking man had trouble turning down a true gold coin as this . . .

The banker really didn't want to sell him for twenty bucks, but rolled the gold coin around in his hand, it felt good to him, it was smooth, a greedy man has a hard time giving up a genuine gold coin . . . "He's worth more, but well, I am too busy to get the good out of him anyway" . . . He penned a quick bill of sale and signed it . . . But unknowingly he kept fondling the gold coin in his hand . . . Wade knew that greed had won over good common sense . . .

Wade returned to the livery stable and showed his bill of sale and gave Jim two bits for a halter and lead rope, and took his purchase and headed back out of town . . . He wanted to be back home, so they rode at a good pace, the sorrel was feeling fresh and ready to put ground under his belly, the black horse he had just bought moved out easily with them, the rope around his neck barely felt tension as he kept the same pace . . . Riding into the barn lot going on midnight, Wade unsaddled his sorrel and turned him into the corral and started to fetch down some hay for them, but Ramos was already a step ahead of him, as he was inspecting the new horse, it was easy to see that Ramos had a way with horses, as he ran his hands over the horse checking every bone in his body . . . He smiles at Wade: "A fine animal, young, full of fire, strong and solid in every way" . . . He greatly approved . . .

Wade took pride in his choice as well, and surprised they found as good a horse flesh as this . . . He was impressed with how Ramos was handling the horse, it was easy to see that he had been around many a horse before and knew just how to calm them . . . Running his hands over the horses entire body in a soothing relaxing way, talking gently, in Spanish, the horse seemed to nearly fall asleep as Ramos inspected him . . .

Mary had heard Wade ride in and was at the barn standing beside him, a heavy cotton flannel type robe pulled around her body, her hair pulled back and tied with a strip of cloth, she smiles as she see how intently Ramos goes over the horse as well . . . "Wade, you must be tired and exhausted from so much riding today, would you like me to brew a fresh pot of coffee"?

"No, all I want right now is to wash off some of this earth and hit that sack" . . . They turned to go to the house, but Ramos stayed rubbing his hands over the new horse . . . "Thank you señor, I thank you over and over, you have no idea señor" . . .

Wade turns back and smiles: "He's yours, you paid for him with your own money, all I did was go fetch him, I can't wait till the sun comes up and see if you can ride him" . . .

"I will not disappoint you my friend"

"No, I don't figure you will, get some rest, we will check him out when the sun rises" . . .

The night seemed short as Wade rolled out of bed just as the sun was peering through a crack in the doorway, Mary had beat him out of bed and already had a fresh brew on the fire, holding him a hot cup, Wade took the cup and took a deep sip, and swirled it around in his mouth, the fresh aroma of it smelled good and seemed to make the day seem brighter already, bacon had already been searing in the skillet with some fresh biscuits and jam set along beside it on the rough cut table, it seemed that Mary was as anxious to check out the new horse as he was . . .

Mary opened the door to holler for Ramos, for breakfast was ready, but Ramos was already working with the new black horse, he had him on a lead rope, working in short circles then letting slack in the rope and moving him farther out, then pulling him back in and then changing directions, Ramos would make him change stride and lead with the commands of his voice . . . It was obvious that he had worked horses before and the black horse picked up quickly on what was asked of him . . . The black horse had the look of intelligence in his eyes, that was one thing that Wade always noticed when looking over horses, he was a strong horse but sleek in conformation, signs of speed rippled in his muscle tone, he was solid black but had a white star and a snip on his head, with two white socks on the rear . . . Ramos claimed he was not hungry as he continued working with him . . .

Wade and Mary had finished their breakfast and headed out the door, stepping off the porch Wade swallowed the last sip of coffee he wanted and tossed the remainder of what was in the cup to the ground and set the cup on the edge of the porch . . . They walked across the dirt yard and to the corral, Ramos was rubbing an old wool blanket on the horse, then gently laid it across his back, he tied the lead rope in a loop around the horse's neck to be used as reigns . . . Wade stepped in the corral to help him upon the horse, but before Wade got the gate closed, Ramos had swung up on his back as a young kid might have done, Wade simply shook his head and stepped back out of the corral . . . "If you need any help, just holler" . . .

Ramos simply smiled and nodded his hat as he passed by at leisurely trot . . . The horse was stepping right out with ease under the confidence of his rider . . .

Wade and Mary retrieved their horses and saddled up and the three of them headed out into the valley, with a yelp, Roscoe trailed along as well, chasing an occasional rabbit along the way, but wouldn't chase them far for fear he would get left behind and miss something . . .

They rode through to the far end of the valley and climbed the trail up to the higher valley, Wade wanted to check things out better up there . . . Water and grass would be a plenty for summer grazing up here he thought to himself . . . He was ready to get his herd . . . After some discussion, they decided they needed to get things ready and head south to where Ramos knew of the loose cattle, cattle that had been brought from Mexico and scattered by the Apache, cattle that had been running wild in the rugged lava plains and plateaus . . .

Wade set on the porch as the evening sun barely showing itself above the horizon, casting orange shadows amongst what little clouds drifted slightly in the evening breeze, Wade smiling to himself and almost broke into an all out laugh, Mary had just stepped to the door, and caught him with a smile on his face . . . "And what has your spirits so joyful Mr. Tavner"?

Wade's eyes had a gleam in them as he looks up at Mary, "A year ago, I had nothing but a saddle, a colt and Winchester, not a care in the world but to watch my own backside, no one to stop me from doing anything I set my sights on, now, I have the best looking woman in the world beside me, a dog, and I reckon I now have a grandfather, what could be next"? Roscoe just picked up his coffee cup and took off with it in his teeth, jumping out in the dirt yard, growling, trying to get Wade to try to get it from him . . . Wade simply looked up at Mary, shaking his head "He's your dog, remember, your dog" . . .

Mary laughed back at him: "But it's your coffee cup" . . .

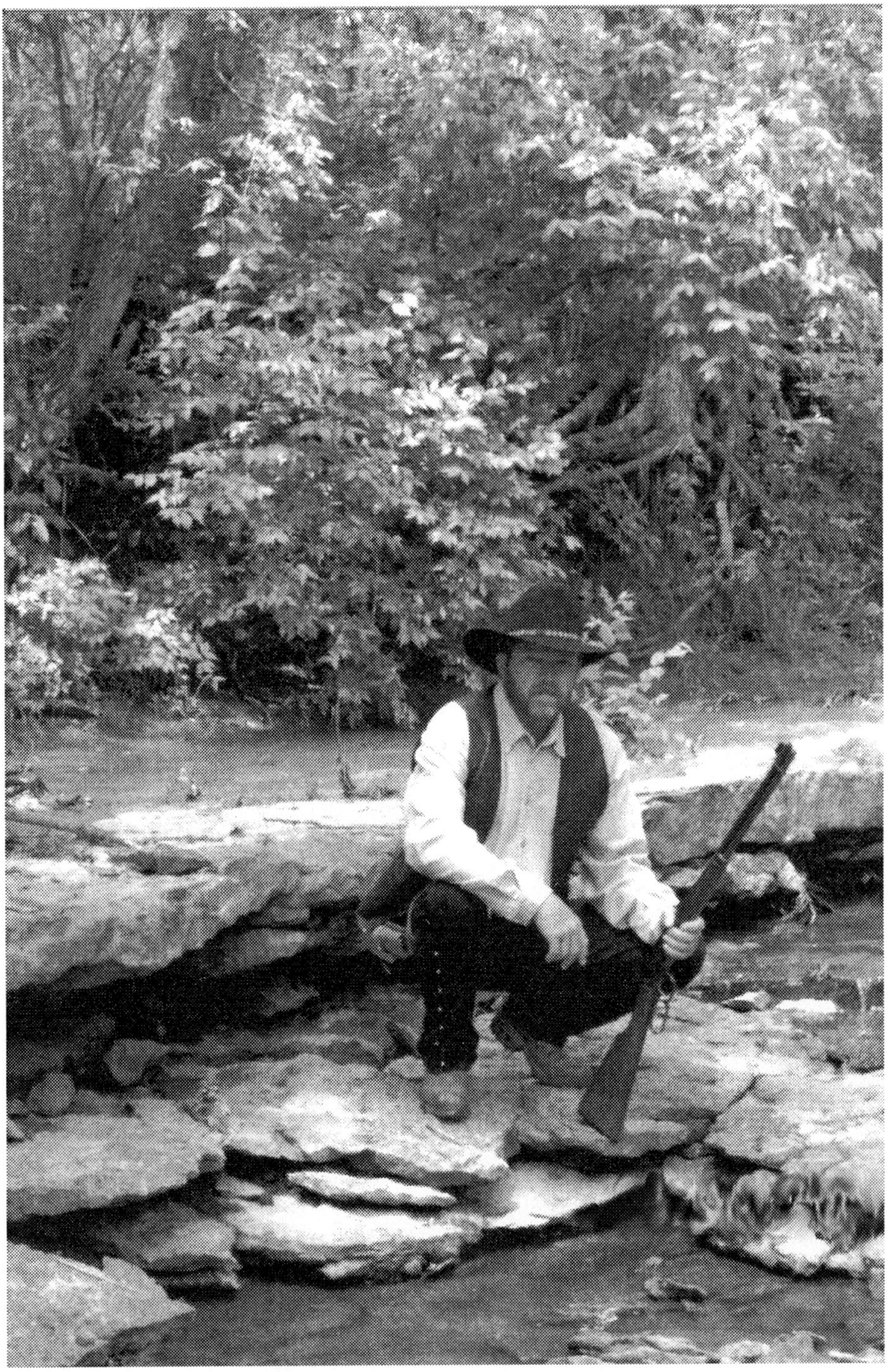

Chapter 9

Plans had been made to leave early and head south and west to the place of where Ramos knew of the cattle . . . Ramos had told Wade of the area, Wade was slightly aware of the area, but it was an area most travelers avoided because it was a rough, hard to travel country and not much of any reason to cross it, it was much easier to get where ever you were going by simply going around that stretch of wilderness, what trails lead into the area were hard to find and very rocky, the lava rock outcroppings were dangerous as they were jagged and sharp, hard on a horse and rider, the ground being loose with lava stone, a slip in the wrong area and horse and rider wouldn't make it out . . .

Ramos lead out after a quick breakfast and possibles stashed away in the saddlebags . . . Saddles were loaded with as much as they could hold, two burlap bags thrown over Ramos's horses flanks as he had no saddle or saddle bags . . . They had rode for several hours and had stopped for a bite to eat, jerky and biscuits, water was dipped from a nearby stream from a tin cup that they all shared . . .

They skirted around the western slopes, Ramos was looking deep into the woods as they rode, stopping occasionally to look into the landscape, finally reigning up, sliding down from his black horse and motioning for Wade and Mary to do the same, tying the horses amongst the trees, they climb the steep embankment a good hundred feet or more, leaving them half breathless, topping out into an opening on the side of the mountain, it was a level place right on the side of the slope, brush had grown thick, so thick it was hard to push your way through, scrub oak type of brush, they pushed their way back a good fifty feet, it was a place nearly dark, the tall pines on the slope let little sun through and the brush took care of the rest, Ramos stopped and pointed towards the wall of the mountain, "This was my home for many years", as he reached down and pulled some dead limbs away from the stone face of the mountain and revealed a cave that was nearly hidden from view, Wade had to duck his head to clear the rock overhang, at the entrance of the cave it seemed dark and damp, but as a man walked deeper into the darkness, his eyes became more adjusted to what little light there was . . . The dampness had given away to dry dirt floors back into the cave . . . Ramos struck a match and lit a clump of burlap that had been wrapped tightly around a stick, apparently soaked in fat or resin of some kind as it burned brightly, walking farther into the cave they came upon a larger room in the cave, the room must have been a good twenty feet in diameter, they must have been a good hundred feet into the cave, set about in this room were a log made chair and a hammock of a bed, a fire pit and a few odds and ends cooking utensils, over in the corner, Ramos reached down and pulled back a buffalo hide that was nearly hidden from view, not only because of the darkness but had been sifted over with dirt, so to blend in with the landscape, lying there on the ground lie a spanish saddle, a saddle horn twice the size of Wade's, but what caught the eye even more were the silver rowels that were fastened all along the sides of it, a leather braided rope lay on top of it, a fine tooled set of saddle bags as well, and an ole walker pistol, Ramos looks at them and smiles, "This is all I have left in this world, I have kept this hidden for many years for I know that some men would kill me simply for my saddle" . . .

Wade reaches down and hoists the saddle up on his back and they haul the cache back to the horses, Wade tosses the saddle up on the black horse and checks all the billets and cinch, tightens it up and admires the workmanship of the saddle, they unload the burlap bags from his horse into the saddlebags . . . Ramos climbs into the saddle and a grin engulfs his entire face, "We are ready to go get your cattle Señor Wade" . . .

They ride down off the western slopes of the range and head into some high plains areas, the sun had starting dropping below the distant horizon and the temperatures were falling with it, Wade pulls into one of the last clumps of aspen trees and steps from his sorrel, stretching his back and legs, as it's been a long ride today . . . Camp is quickly set up, a fire kindled into flames, Ramos was gathering more wood for the fire and Wade walks back into camp carrying a jackrabbit and a sage grouse . . . Ramos quickly takes both from Wade and walks out a ways from camp and cleans them both, but comes back and hands Mary the grouse, "Much better eating" . . . Ramos goes out into the plains and cuts open a cactus, and peels back the needles on it and cuts out the fresh meat under the skin and they sear it in with the grouse . . . It was a good meal, and they were all full . . .

The sun had dropped below the distant range, casting it's remnants of shadows long on the earth, which were soon engulfed in the darkness of the night, the fire flickered into the darkness with sparks of embers floating upwards and disappearing into the darkness as well, the smell of wood smoke and of sage drifting in the evening air, the moon was high and nothing more than a crescent shape, the moon appeared to be lying on it's back with both points pointing upwards, Wade looking up towards the moon, "It's a dry moon, that's a good sign for us" . . . Mary lay against Wade, both leaned back against a bed of pine needles and sage with bedrolls stretched out on top, Wade could tell by the way of her breathing that she had already fell asleep, he pulled the bedrolls up around her shoulders and tucked down himself . . . Ramos was fast asleep as well . . . Roscoe was curled up beside Mary, he was tuckered too, he was a full year old now and had made every step along the way, he had grown into a big dog, his head as big as a melon with big soft brown eyes with a black nose and hair a golden yellow . . . Wade swore he was as big as a half grown bear cub . . .

Wade was up well before his companions cracked an eye, the fire was kindled back into a blaze and coffee on, the cracking and popping of the fire aroused them both . . . "Are you two going to sleep the day away"? Ramos quickly jumped up and shook out his bedroll and rolled it up in a tight roll and laced it with rawhide strings, Mary pulled the rough cover back up, "The sun isn't even up yet", Roscoe made a whimpering noise as he had edged his way under Mary's blanket . . .

"The ride to tough for womenfolk"?

Mary pulled the cover away and starts to get up, her hand touches on a pine cone which she grasps and hurls in Wades direction, hitting him square in the back . . .

Wade smiles and hands her the warm cup of fresh coffee, "Don't start something you can't handle ma'am" . . .

"Do I look worried Mr. Tavner"?

Camp was broke and cleaned up, it would be a long ride across the high plain dessert they faced today, the sun would be hot, and little water out in the prairie, they reached the far side with no more than an hour before dark set in, the pine trees had gained a foothold here and were scattered about, with a few springs here and there, a big cottonwood tree loomed towards the sky, where they found fresh water from a good spring, Wade always kept an eye out for cottonwood trees while traveling this type of country, for the cottonwoods always grew where there was moisture, but he would never camp near one if it looked stormy at all, for they seemed to attract lightening also . . . The cool night air felt good after searing out in the sun all day, sleep came easy for them all . . .

Riding out the next morning, the ground seemed to just fall out from under them, it was an area that reminded Wade of what they call the badlands of the Dakotas, the ground had been eroded away and fell into a vast wasted valley of rocks and ancient volcanoes, the rim was miles across in all directions, the trail leading down was narrow and dangerous, and it was obvious, that no one had used this trail in some time, the gray rocks turned into dark brown and nearly black at times, these were the lava flows of another time, rains had washed ditches in and around them, but they were sharp and the going steep, cutting through some of the ravines barely left room for the width of a horse, they had to lift their legs up to keep from crushing them or cutting them against the sides, trees were scarce, but an occasional patch of green grass lie on top of the pinnacles that dotted the landscape . . . Farther into this barren wasteland though, showed signs of larger areas of green grass, it seemed even greener against this barren dark colored wasteland . . .

They had seen a couple of signs of tracks, tracks made by cattle, and an occasional track of a coyote, riding around a bend in the canyon, revealed a large area of broken valleys, valleys lined with lush green grass, water holes scattered about, and long horned cattle roaming freely about, cattle that had been here for generations of their original owners, cattle that had survived the hardships of this country, but also a cattle that had been neglected as there were calves of all ages here . . . Riding out amongst the cattle, most of them scattered into the brush lined slopes, within minutes all of them had disappeared but a few older cows and bulls that felt no danger enough to run . . . Cattle of all sizes and color roamed here . . . Wade smiled, but also thought of what a feat this would be to move all these cattle out through the trail they just rode in on . . . Riding from different patches of broken valleys, the longhorns were numbered in the hundreds, and that was just the ones they could see, who knows how many are already lined in the brushy slopes . . .

Wade looked at Ramos: "Is there another trail in or out of here" . . .

"No señor, the trail we used getting here is all there is" . . .

Mary could see the worried look on Wades face: "Let's make camp on top of one of these pinnacles where we can watch them from above, we can tie the horses below near the water, it's late and we are all tired and hot, give ourselves a good nights rest to think on it" . . .

They picketed their horses close to the water with an area of good grass for them to eat on, then climbed upon a pinnacle of rock with a plateau of not more than thirty feet wide, but even here the grass was green, Wade let down his rope and went back down and scrounged up wood and tied it to the rope and Mary would pull it up until they had enough wood for the night . . . As evening crept in, the view from their perch was magnificent, the air cooled down and the longhorns ventured out of the shady slopes into the grassy valleys, the entire valley changed it's appearance right before your eyes as the shadows stretched long and the colors of the rocks and pinnacles changed with the moving sunlight, but as the sun dropped, darkness quickly took over . . . The fire felt good as they set around contemplating their strategies to move these cattle out of this oasis of valleys . . . The yap of a lone coyote echoed into the darkness of the night . . . Their fire seemed to glow against the backdrop of the other pinnacles scattered about, casting it's own shadows . . .

Wade was up well before the crack of dawn, setting close to the edge of the pinnacle looking down into the valley below, he watched as the cattle moved freely about, spotting cows and calves and many a rangy looking bull, cattle with horns nearly four feet on each side of their skulls . . .

They had decided to start at the southern most valley and push the cattle towards the north and to the highest valley where the trail led out into the high plains, if they could get them herded into the north valley, then push them harder, the ones at the north end of the valley would have to move up the thin trail as pressure was put on them, it was a risky attempt, hoping they wouldn't bolt and stampede back towards them, their lives would be in extreme danger if that was to happen . . .

Sliding back down from their lofty perch above, they saddled their horses, leaving bedrolls and anything else here at the base, only their ropes and canteens and Wades Winchester were to be taken . . . Skirting south along the east slope as far as they could, until they reached the far south end, then spreading out along the sides of the grassy valleys, pushing the cattle through towards the north and into the next valley, the cattle were skittish of them and pushing them now was easy work, Roscoe joined in as he would run and nip at their heels when the opportunity existed, then looking back at Wade for approval of his job well done . . .

The first two days of pushing the cattle had gone well, but the farther north they went, the rougher the terrain got, and the size of the herd getting bigger all the time . . . Each morning they would have to go back south and push back north as the cattle would move back behind them during the night . . .

Ramos was working the eastern slope as it was much easier for one person, Wade and Mary and Roscoe were working the west side, the terrain here was much wider and rocky, with small pockets of ravines and ridges, some blocked off box canyons of two to three hundred feet . . . Wade and Mary would try keeping a distance of no more than a hundred yards between them, and Roscoe would run in between keeping the cattle from escaping between them . . .

Mary rounded a bend and rode into a small canyon looking for strays, the entrance wasn't more than ten feet wide, but she had seen tracks leading into it, Wade had lost sight of her, but pushing a good group of his own out into the open valley, Mary had rode into the small canyon a good hundred yards and realized there was no way out but the way she rode in, it had got narrow and tight with rocks nearly straight up in the back, jagged rocks protruded out from the sides . . . Roscoe was behind her, and she heard him growling, turning her horse around she stood facing one of the biggest rangiest looking longhorn bulls she had seen, and he wasn't running, he had squared off for a fight, Roscoe was raising a ruckus like he'd never done, he knew trouble was at hand, the hair on his back was standing straight up like a razor back hog . . . Mary was trapped, her horse next to panic, she had a tight reign on him and the other hand had a death grip on the saddle horn, the horse spun in a tight circle a couple of times, but there was no way out, the bull was pawing the ground tossing dirt way over his back, blowing snot out his nose, head low to the ground, impending the coming charge, Mary screamed at the top of her lungs for Wade . . .

    Wade had become worried since he hadn't seen Mary for some time, and was working in that direction, pulling up reign on his sorrel, he could hear Roscoe raising a fit, but he was over on the other side of this rock wall, looking back south he could see the entrance was more than a good hundred yards away, the wall that divided them was a good twenty feet high, then Wade heard the panic in Mary's cry for help, it was a blood curdling scream, calling his name . . . He peeled from his horse, Winchester sliding from the scabbard in one slick motion, climbing the rock barrier as fast as he could get up it, just as he crested the top he saw the bull charge, Roscoe met him halfway, sinking his teeth into the big bulls nose and shaking as hard as he could, the bull backed off momentarily, blood streaming from his nose, and then charged again, Roscoe rushed in to meet him a second time, but the bull took one swipe with his horns and caught Roscoe just behind his left front leg right under his ribs and tossed him into the air, up over some bushes and landing hard on the jagged rocky slope, not a sound came from him, only the thud of him landing on the rocks, the bull then turned towards Mary and charged again, Wades Winchester quickly reached his shoulder as he poured lead into the animal as fast as he could work the lever, five shots into his shoulder and neck, he stopped just short of Mary, blood streaming from his side, lashing with his horns towards his right side from where he felt the pain, making another circle and regaining sight of his target, a frothy breath of blood from his nostrils, getting ready to charge again, Wade put a round into the animals skull, dropping him within feet of Mary's horse, her horse taking a leap over the back end of the bull and wasting no time getting out of the canyon . . . Riding to where Wade's horse was standing, Wade climbed back down from the wall, Mary quickly slid off her horse, nearly collapsing into Wade's arms . . . Pale as a ghost and shaking uncontrollably, tears rolling from her eyes . . . But then with a quick gasp of her breath, she shouted . . . "Roscoe" . . .

    Ramos had just rode up, Wade leaving Mary with him, gathered up his Winchester and mounted his sorrel and quickly headed down and around and back into the canyon, stepping from his horse he heard movement in the bushes, crawling on his hands and knees he found Roscoe lying there, his big brown eyes looking up at Wade, reaching over and running his hand over his head between his ears, looking for any sign of blood, but found none, he picked him up, weighing a good hundred pounds as he was a big dog, Wade carried him out to where Mary was setting on a rock, horse following behind, he laid Roscoe down beside Mary, she quickly drops to her knees beside him and hugs him, tears streaming down her cheeks as Roscoe lays motionless . . . Wade retrieves his canteen from the saddle and props Roscoe's head up and gently pours a small amount of water in his mouth, Roscoe works his tongue and quickly laps it up, within half an hour he is setting up and has an alert look in his eyes, head still resting in Mary's lap, her stroking his thick fur nonstop . . .

Wade smiles at them, "He'll be just fine as soon as you quit babying him, just had the wind knocked out of himself" . . .

"I'll quit babying him when I feel like it, he earned it" . . .

Wade gathers up the reigns on his horse, "I'll go get the camp gear, we might as well make camp right here tonight" . . .

Ramos pulled a knife from his belt, Wade looked at him with question in his eyes . . . Ramos smiles back, "We are eating beef tonight my friend, you shot him, I'll go get us some steak for the fire tonight" . . .

They set around the fire, bellies full, none of them had eaten beef for some time, a beef steak charred over an open fire was a hard meal to beat, it was a far sight from the rabbits and grouse and venison they'd been living on, the old bull was a bit tough, but the flavor was superb . . . Roscoe ate his fill as well . . .

The next two days they had pushed the cattle to the far north end of the broken valleys, tomorrow they would herd them up and try to push them into the thin trail leading out and to the high plains meadows . . . This worried Wade for fear of them stampeding back over them, but it was the only way to get them out . . .

Morning rolled around and a quick breakfast put away, saddles were thrown on and bedrolls and all belongings tied on, they worked the cattle back towards the far end as they had wandered out grazing during the night hours, once they were all gathered and pushed to the far end, they started crowding the outside bunches, which pushed against the cattle to the rear, things were starting to get explosive when Ramos hollered: "They are going, they are heading up the trail" . . . Sure enough, as soon as the first few found the opening and started up, they poured into it, it was like sand running through a funnel, it took nearly three hours to get the last ones up . . . Once the cattle were up on the high plains plateau, they spread out like a herd of buffalo . . . It was a sight to see, as the three of them set in their saddles in amazement, both because the herd looked so good stretching out before them and because they had pulled it off, getting them out of the hidden oasis below . . . It was like a huge sigh of relief . . .

It was three weeks before they rounded the north end of their valley and turned the cattle into some of the richest grass they had seen, it was a long dry drive getting here, Wade and Ramos set up the log rails that blocked off the north entrance to their valley, the cattle had spread throughout the valley in no time, hundreds of them lined the crystal clear creek that ran down the west side, drinking their fill, it was as though they knew too, this was home . . .

They rode back through the cattle heading to the cabin, it was a sight for sore eyes, it was home . . . It was home for them all, Wade, Mary, Ramos and Roscoe . . . .

Chapter 10

Wade felt like summer was half over by the time they got their cattle herded home, yet there were so many things yet to do . . .

They worked hard for weeks, separating the younger cows and young stock and moving them to the high meadows above, the grass rubbed on the bellies of the cows and was lush from the melting snows, water was fresh and cold in the higher valleys . . . There were way too many bulls running in the group, so they had thinned them out and took the best ones to the higher valley with the young stock, leaving one bull to thirty cows . . . The remainder of the older cows and bulls were left in the lower valley, the older cows would do better here with less competition for food and water and Wade intended to run the remaining bulls and leftovers out into the plains north of their valley . . .

Ramos was with them to stay, they knew that, and wanted it no other way, as he had become a great help and had become a part of their family, he was the grandfather they neither one had ever had . . . Wade and Ramos had added another room on the back of the cabin, Ramos had never asked why they were building on to it, as he felt it none of his business . . . The day they finished the room, Wade informed him that this was his room, he was part of their family, tears streamed down the cheeks of his face . . . Ramos wanted to thank them from the full of his heart, but couldn't speak as his emotions had overtaken him, Mary walked over to him and put her arms around him and just held him tight . . . No words were needed . . . Wade even felt a little choked up himself . . . Roscoe set in the doorway, brown eyes a glow, tail wagging the back end of his body . . .

The remainder of the summer was spent cutting poles and building corrals . . . Wade would leave shortly after sunup each morning and ride into the high valley and check the herd up there, some mornings Mary would ride with him, but Roscoe never missed a chance to get out and run, he was Mary's dog, but he stayed at Wade's side and never missed going to check on the cows . . . Ramos would dig a couple of post holes while Wade was checking cows, then when he returned he would do the digging of holes and Ramos would set posts, Mary would help Ramos with the setting up posts and poles, Wade felt as though he was being worked to hard and out numbered . . . But he got no sympathy only maybe from Roscoe . . .

Wade would ride out of the evenings and check the cattle in the lower valley, Mary would be watching for Wade to ride back across the valley late in the evenings, she felt there was nothing better than seeing Wade set his horse, loping across the valley as the sun was setting in the western horizon, it made a warm feeling that ran through her entire body . . .

About every third day, the three of them would ride out into the open plains north of their valley and check on the herd of renegade bulls and culls, this land did not belong to them, but worked good for it's purpose, it was open range here . . . The grass was not near as good and plentiful out here either, and water more scarce as well . . . They would spend the day pushing this bunch to fresher grass and bunching them back up, there were also buffalo that roamed here . . .

Summer had nearly passed, the aspen trees were taking on a yellowish hue . . . Supplies would be needed before winter set in . . . A trip to Silver Creek Springs was in order . . . Wade informed them they would be driving the herd out north into town, they were animals of no use to them, the culls and over stock of bulls . . .

Ramos really had no desire to go back into Silver Creek Springs, but he knew that Wade and Mary would need help driving that bunch of cattle . . .

Wade knew that the only meat being served in town was venison and bear and felt for sure that he could sell this small herd there . . . There were close to a hundred head of cattle, and not an easy bunch to move, so it would be more than the normal ten hours of riding . . .

It was early of the morning as they saddled up and headed out the north end of their valley and proceeded to round up the rogue bunch and head them west towards Silver Creek Springs . . . It was a hard task as the bulls weren't good drivers and were always testing their luck at getting back around behind them, and if one could sneak back around others would break away too . . .

Three and half days later they could see the edge of town in sight, the livery stables were on the west side of town, and the only corrals anywhere around . . . Wade went ahead and rented the corrals from the livery . . . Luckily Jim Wilson had increased the size of the corrals to keep up with the growth of the town . . . Wade helped him move a few horses and three mules to a smaller pen behind the barn . . . He told Jim that he had beef and they were to be sold to the highest bidder . . . He then rode back out of town and met Mary and Ramos, he originally had planned on taking them north of town and bringing them in from the west side of town, but the more he thought about it, he might as well take them right down the main street so everyone in town knew there was beef available . . . They brought them right through the main street, miners had lined the boardwalks in awe watching the cattle meander right through town, horns rattling against the other making a clattering sound that muffled any conversations . . .

The word had spread through town that Wade was going to sell them . . . Wade was figuring to get around fifteen dollars a head, but was hoping for maybe seventeen or even eighteen, . . . There were three diners in town now, and Wade had noticed riding through town that all three had nothing but deer and bear on the chalkboard slates out front, these miners would be wanting beef . . . The town had grown to double its size since the last time they were in town, and all the tent businesses had wood framed store fronts now . . .

The crowd had gathered around at the livery stables as they pushed the last one in, Jim swung the gate shut behind them . . . Jim looked up at Wade: "Didn't know there was any beef around these parts anywhere, sure going to enjoy me a steak" . . .

Wade announced the bidding would start at ten o'clock sharp tomorrow morning . . . After forking over a few piles of loose hay to keep them settled down, the three of them headed for Mabry's Eatery, they were all hungry . . . Wade stepped in the doorway and stopped momentarily to let his eyes adjust to the light of the room, He picked out a table at the far end of the room and proceeded to it, a table he could keep his back to the wall and a view out the doorway into main street, Mary a step behind him, but when he reached the table, Ramos was not along with them, Wade helped Mary with her chair then went to check on Ramos . . . Ramos was setting on the edge of the boardwalk just down from the doorway with Roscoe by his feet . . .

Ramos looked up at Wade: "Señor, I am not allowed in this place, I must stay out here or I will cause you much trouble, I fear that Roscoe would have more luck getting fed than me" . . .

Wade reached down and put his hand under Ramos's shoulder and helped him to his feet, "You will eat in here with us or no one will be eating" . . .

"Señor, it is not worth the trouble" . . .

"The heck it ain't, if it's not good enough for you, then we'll go elsewhere" . . .

Ramos truly didn't want to confront the issue . . . Wade walked back through the doorway with Ramos beside him, looking around the room he quickly spotted Bill Mabry, walking directly towards him . . .

Just as Wade approached Mabry, he casually moved his duster to the side exposing the colt that hung from his right hip . . .

"Sir, my friend here thinks that he may not be welcome here, I would hope by all means that there isn't a lick of truth to that" . . .

Bill Mabry had a flush feeling that seemed to creep up around the collar of his shirt and he felt that for sure Wade could see the red coloring of his skin that followed the feeling, but quickly trying his best to clear his throat: "Well why would he think a thing like that"?

"I expect he has his reasons why he would think a thing such as that, but I don't see any reason he wouldn't get served as well as myself" . . .

"No sir Mr. Tavner, he may set at your table if that is what you wish" . . .

"It is" . . .

Venison roast was the special for the day, and they all were all full as ticks, but Wade and Ramos both finished dinner off with a piece of wild berry pie . . .

By ten o'clock the next morning, word had traveled to every miner in the mountains that cattle were to be sold this morning, by nine thirty there was a crowd gathering around the livery, miners were gathered in groups of four and more, pooling their earnings, wanting to buy a beef they could split to butcher, as winter was not far away . . .

At ten o'clock Wade climbed to the loft of the livery stable where he could see out over the crowd, it seemed that nearly every person in town was here, He got their attention and announced that any person could buy one or as many as they wished, and the bidding started . . .

Wade set the bid in at seven dollars a head, and that got them all going, the bid quickly went to nineteen dollars by Bill Mabry, the miners feared he would take them all and would sell the beef to them at three times the price in his restaurant . . . Bill Mabry owned part of the prairies north of town and could turn them out after buying them, Bill figured if he could get them all bought, then he would be the only eating establishment for miles in any direction that had beef on it's menu and would surely put the others out of business, and he had the money backing to do it . . .

One miner in a group of seven men jumped up and shouted: "We'll give you twenty seven bucks" . . .

Bill Mabry could feel that flush feeling coming over him again, and he could feel the sweat starting to protrude on his forehead . . .

Wade looking around over the crowd, "Bidding all done"?

It was silent, "Sold, take what you want, pay the pretty lady standing at the gate" . . .

They quickly stepped over and roped two of the biggest ones in the bunch, and handed Mary a leather bag, "It's pure silver ma'am, should be enough to cover it" . . .

Mary looked up at Wade: "The mans word is good enough for me, anyone else want one at this price"?

Four other groups of miners took what they wanted, paying the same as the first . . .

After all the miners had gotten what they wanted there was only the town folks left . . . Then it was between the owners of the three diners in town . . . Bill Mabry finally got the bid at nineteen dollars and two bits per head . . . Bill had to meet Wade at the bank to arrange the payment, and offered them a meal at his place on him for Wade and Mary and Ramos to drive them out to his ranch north of town . . .

Wade and Mary had twenty one hundred dollars now in a bank account, money needed to stake their ranch on . . . It was more money than Wade had ever had at any one time in his entire life, and he had never had a bank account before, they kept out the hundred dollars and used it buying supplies that would be needed for winter and Wade picked out two new shirts for Mary and got himself a new shirt and a denim pair of britches and a new pair of boots, and they also got Ramos a new pair of boots as his were about to fall apart and also got him a heavy coat for winter . . . When they stepped out and gave him his new things, he couldn't even speak, his eyes were watered up and a lump had caught in his throat and left him unable to speak . . . Roscoe always set patiently outside the doorway waiting for them . . .

The evening was cool as the sun had dropped below the horizon, they entered Mabry's place and ordered supper and started with cups of hot coffee, Wade had chosen the same table again . . . Setting over their evening meal, Wade mentioned that there was now an assay office and land office in town, and wondered about the open prairie that lay north of their valley and how well it worked for running a herd of what was to be sold . . .

After a good nights sleep and a hot breakfast of eggs and deer sausage and biscuits and gravy, they headed towards the livery to saddle their horses and head home . . . Walking past the land office, Mary asked: "Aren't you going to check on the prairie land"?

"It was just a thought Mary" . . .

"And what if some one else buys it before you decide, do I need to hold the door open for you and lead you in"?

"Alright, we can go in and check out how things lie in the area" . . .

It was a small office, one desk pushed out away from the wall just enough for a man to get in behind it, a big map of the area took up nearly all the wall on the left of the office and on the right side were file drawers and cabinets and leather bound ledgers . . . A small man, wearing gray britches with black suspenders reaching over his shoulders, a white shirt under the suspenders with a short thin black bow tie around the collar, a balding fellow wearing small wire framed glasses to which he appeared to peak over the top of when looking at you . . . He stuck out his hand: "The names George Waller" . . .

Wade found their valley on the large map and inquired of the open prairie that lay north of it . . .

"That land has had no claim on it as of yet, and not likely it will as it doesn't appear to be any sort of mining capabilities on it" . . .

Wade ran his finger around an area from the creek out to some foothills and back to their valley, "What would it cost a man to purchase that"?

George took a measuring tool and ran a circumference around Wade's layout, "There would be a thousand acres in there, The government has set a precedence of six dollars an acre out here" . . .

"Six dollars an acre, that's thieving folks a might don't ya think"?

"It's not my say sir, you would have to take that up with the government folks back east, they are calling the shots" . . .

Wade was about ready to walk out as the little man from the bank stepped in . . . "The man with the cattle in the area, thinking of buying some more land to go with that valley of yours"?

Wade did not trust this little man, he didn't trust him simply from his looks, but there was something else he was unaware of that made him just dislike this man . . . Thoughts came to Wade, how did this banker know where their valley was, he had not been there that he knew of . . .

"Mr. Tavner, my bank would be willing to loan you the money you need to buy more land for your ranch, why you have a third of it already in the account you just opened" . . .

"Well we will think on it for a spell and get back with you" . . .

As they walked out and headed for the horses, Mary grabbed Wade's arm and stopped him . . . "It's your decision, but I think you should buy it, you will kick yourself if you don't and some one else does, they could even block us off from going through there" . . .

Wade knew she was right, he just hadn't planned on spending such a large sum of money . . . Walking back into the land office, the banker man was still there as well, "What kind of terms we talking here, say I put a thousand down on that piece of ground, what are the terms"?

"All you will need to do is lay claim to it here, then come to my office and we will set you up and get you approved and once that is done, you come back here and settle with Mr. Waller here and the place is yours" . . .

"You fellows make it sound pretty simple, how much and when do I have to repay the note" . . .

"Mr. Tavner, we will work you out a simple plan on whatever terms you desire" . . .

Wade had a very uneasy feeling . . . "I don't even recollect your name" . . .

"It would be Wesley Simmons" as the banker holds out his hand towards Wade . . .

Terms were agreed on and Wade would make a once a year payment in the fall of every year for five years . . . Wade went from a very uneasy feeling to a great feeling of pride, but also knew he owed a man money, something he had never experienced before . . .

Walking back to the livery stable, Wade looked over the horses Jim had for sale in the lot behind the barn, Jim had just brought these horses in, they had come from the east, seven in all, Wade looking them over picked out three new horses and bartered with Jim and paid for them with some of the pure silver that had been paid to him on some of the cattle deals, and took them home, one being a big tall long legged Palomino gelding, a horse that could cover a lot of ground with easy strides, another one being a bay gelding, a little shorter in height, but a solid built horse with strong muscular hind quarters and a thick chest with a good wide stance, a good horse for roping for branding days, the third horse another sorrel like the one he rode, another solid horse for daily chores . . . They climbed into the saddles and headed east towards home, leading the string of new horses, Ramos approved of Wades choice of horseflesh, Mary had been eyeing the sorrel on her own and was all smiles when Wade bought him too . . .

Nothing felt better than riding back into their valley, cattle wandering out into the lush grass of the valley, the sun just barely peaking above the granite walls on the west side, shadows casting well out into the valley, the temperatures dropping quickly with the setting of the sun, aspens glowing on the eastern slopes as the last of the sun's rays touched the flickering of the golden leaves . . .

There were areas at the south end of the valley where they had kept the cattle off, and had spent days cutting the tall grass with scythes and stacking it with pitch forks in large piles and building pole fences around them, saving it for the worst of the winter days . . . They had hauled long stem grass back to the barn and filled the loft for the horses, pitching it up and packing it down by walking on it . . . The bulls had been removed from the herd and turned out on the prairies north of the valley, Wade wanted to get the herd synchronized to having all spring calves, he would leave the bulls out there until early summer, then turn them back in with the cows so there would be no winter calving, this was no country to be having calves in the cold winter months . . . The remainder of the fall was spent cutting and stacking wood for the winter as well . . . It was a hard life, but one that none of them complained of . . .

Chapter 11

The winter months had been endured, the cattle grazed in the lower valley throughout the winter, they had fed all but two of the piles of hay they had stacked up . . . The grass had fresh green shoots protruding through, the buds on the aspens seemed to open up over night, wild flowers dotted the eastern slopes where the sun reached early of the morning warming the ground quickly, the stream behind the cabin ran at full bank as the snows of the high peaks were melting away, the water being clear and cold . . . Calving season had begun and kept them all busy checking cattle throughout the day, Wade watched after the momma cows with diligence, taking up the biggest portion of the day . . . Mary loved watching the new babies bound around in the valley floor and loved the way Wade watched over their herd . . . Ramos was a good hand at tending the cattle as well, Roscoe learned quickly that momma cows with new babies didn't like dogs and that horns were sharp and hooves hurt, he was demoted to staying at the cabin on most outings in the early spring while the babies were being born . . .

It had been nearly three years since they had settled in this valley and brought cattle to these parts . . .

Wade had developed a reputation among the folks of Silver Creek Springs, a reputation of being a fare man, a man who treated others with the same due respect, but also the reputation of the man quick with a gun who stood for what was right to every man, every person in the area knew of the killing of Billy Slade a couple of years earlier, word like that traveled fast and lingered long afterwards . . .

Three Valleys Ranch had become known to all of the area, a clientele of buyers of their cattle had been established with the miners and eating establishments of town . . . Miners frequently came out to the ranch and bought one or two head for butchering, and Wade always accommodated them with an equal price to all at twenty dollars a head, but often reneged on his standard price for those he knew couldn't afford the amount . . . There had been a few families that had moved into the area, with one young couple with two little boys that had staked a claim on some ranch land a good fifty miles west of Silver Creek Springs . . . They had rode to Three Valleys Ranch with enough cash money to buy thirty head of stock to start their own ranch . . . Wade and Mary ran a couple extra head in the group and offered them the loan of a good bull to go with them . . . Wade was always willing to let any man or boy willing enough to work for it to work off twenty dollars in labor for a beef, there was plenty of work to be done on the ranch, from scything hay, to building fences and corrals or cutting wood . . .

Their herd had grown more than what could be sold locally here in the area, time had come to drive a herd of yearlings and two year olds to the markets south and east of Silver Creek Springs, to the rail heads or possibly Denver . . . Only the best heifers were kept for stock cows or replacement of older cows, there were a good number of steers and culled heifers running on the open range north of the valley . . .

Wade and Mary had decided that Wade would go to town and find three or four young men willing to work if he could, to help him with the drive . . . The drive would take a good month and maybe longer to get the cattle that far, Mary and Ramos would stay at the ranch and tend the cows here, the cows would be in the upper valley by mid summer with plenty of grazing and water . . .

Wade left early of the morning and headed to Silver Creek Springs, arriving late afternoon, going to the livery stable first and discussed with Jim Wilson whether he knew of any young men wanting a job for a couple of months or so . . . He mentioned a name or two . . . Wade wandered to the general store and inquired of the folks there as well, these were mostly mining people, but new folks had come to the area lately . . . Wade left word around town for any men looking for work to meet him at the Wilson's Livery at nine o'clock sharp tomorrow morning . . .

At eight o'clock there were four young men looking for work, three of whom had their own horse, the fourth lanky fella was on foot . . . Waiting until nine was fruitless, as this was it . . .

Wade surveyed them over, "The job will pay thirty dollars for a month" . . . Wade quickly could tell that none of these boys had ever had thirty dollars in their pockets, as smiles broke out across their faces . . . They were young men, not one of them over twenty he didn't figure, and none of them had ever drove cattle, but were all eager to earn a man's wages . . .

Wade looked at the lanky kid with no horse: "You got something to ride kid"?

"No sir, I don't, but I would be willing to work for a horse, maybe you could pay me twenty dollars in advance and I could get me a horse and you pay me what's due me at the end"?

Wade looked at Jim Wilson, who was setting on the top rail of the corral, giving him a hidden wink: "You got a twenty dollar horse this man could buy"?

"Well I got horses, but twenty dollars don't buy much of a horse, I got one around back green broke and looks like he's got some mule in him" . . .

The lanky kid had a look of desperation on his face, he wanted to work, he wanted a horse, it was obvious the kid was dirt poor . . .

Wade untied the lariat from his saddle: "Son, can you throw a loop"?

"Well I will surely try sir, I learn fast I tell ya"

Wade tosses his lariat to him: "Well you walk in that corral there and you see if you can rope the horse that you think is the best one in there, we'll settle with Jim afterwards" . . .

The kid walked in the corral and looked them over one by one, then a second look around and passed on a couple then stretched out his rope and tossed a loop over the head of a roan gelding, he didn't have a lot of mane or tail, but a good solid horse, Wade thought to himself, probably the one I'd of took too . . .

The kid led his choice out of the pen shutting the gate behind him . . .

Wade stepped over and run his hands over the horse, feeling his legs and joints, then running his hand over his withers and under his girth, then looking at the kid: "Where's your saddle son"?

"Well I don't rightly have one" . . .

"Jim, you got a saddle you can sell this here fella too"?

"Got a used Calvary saddle in the back room there, it ain't got no saddle horn on it" . . .

The lanky kid was smiling again, looking up at Wade, "Son, you're going to end up owing more money than you might make, maybe Jim here will buy them back from you when you get back" . . .

"No sir, they're going to be mine when I'm done working for you Mr. Tavner" . . . Wade pulls the leather wallet from inside his vest pocket and pays Jim for the horse and saddle . . . "Now does anyone here need to go home and say good bye's to their momma's"? The boys came ready for work and were ready to head out . . .

"Well saddle up boys, we got a ride to make and we can get acquainted on the trail" . . . Wade's sorrel had a good nights rest and a scoop of oats and was ready to hit the trail and head back home so the pace was brisk, it was a good ten hour ride back to Three Valley Ranch and it was close to noon already, Wade pushed them hard just to see what metal they had in their britches . . . Pulling into the ranch yard shortly after dark: "You boys can throw your bedrolls in the barn tonight, unless you'd rather sleep out here under the stars, you might as well get used to that, we got a good month or two of it coming up starting first light tomorrow morning" . . .

Mary walks out and meets each of them and bringing a iron pot of stew with her and a half dozen tin plates . . . Each of them staring at her . . . Wade had just reached over and took the pot to help her as it was heavy as Mary dipped out a good portion and put it on a plate for each of them: "Boys, this here is Mary, and if I catch you boys staring at her again like that, we're going to have words" . . .

Each of them, unaware they had been staring at her, quickly looked down at their plates and dug in, they were not only tired from the days ride, but starved as well . . . .

Wade was up well before daylight, packing as much as he could stash in the saddle bags, Mary had coffee on and breakfast already started, she was nervous about Wade leaving, she wanted to go along too, but she was also glad she wasn't going, but her heart would ache for Wade while he was gone, she knew worry would be a daily thing, her and Ramos and Roscoe would watch over the ranch and cattle while he was gone, it had to be this way . . .

To Wade's surprise when he stepped out on the porch, the four young men he'd hired were up and ready to hit the trail . . . Ramos stood silently by, Wade knew that Ramos had rolled them out of their bedrolls early and had them ready to ride, each man packed with food for several days, a bedroll and a slicker . . .

Wade stepped back upon the porch and kissed Mary goodbye, "We'll see you in a month or two depending on how fast we can drive them and a lot depends on the weather, cattle will only graze so fast" . . . Mary's eyes have welled with tears and her heart seems to be pounding in her throat, she holds on to his hand one last second, she tries to speak, but can't . . . Wade looks into her eyes: "It's ok, we'll be fine and be back before you know it" . . .

"You better Wade Tavner, we will be waiting for you" . . .

Wade reaches down and rubs his hand across the big head of Roscoe, pats him gently between his ears: "You take good care of the place now you hear" . . . The big dog looks up at Wade with those big brown eyes, tail wagging his whole body . . .

Ramos is holding the reigns to Wades sorrel, Wade takes them from him: "Look after Mary while I'm gone, take care my friend" . . .

"Señor, I wish I was riding with you, but I will watch over the ranch for you in your absence, worry about nothing Señor, we will be fine" . . .

Mary has a pit in her stomach as she watches them ride out through the valley and off towards the sunrise . . .

Wade had given each a quick glance over and could read people, he noticed what each person was wearing and how they handled themselves and their horses . . .

Willy Stone was the tall lanky boy and seemed to fit right on his horse, and was eager to prove his worth, he wore a hat that looked a size small and hair sticking out from under it in all directions, his legs seemed to nearly wrap around the belly of his steed, he was the youngest of the boys at no more than sixteen Wade figured, if he was back east he might still be schooling, but out here, sixteen is expected to be a full grown man . . . He carried a small bore rimfire rifle . . . Wade pointed to it strapped to his saddle; "You any good with that cap gun son"?

With a smile that seemed to stretch to each ear: "There ain't no one any better sir" . . .

"Well good, you just got the job of shooting two or three rabbits or squirrels or grouse each day for our supper, you don't get something, we don't eat, simple as that" . . .

"Why you can count on eating Mr. Tavner" . . .

Bob Mocker was a silent fellow, but a man who went about his business with efficiency of a man much older, he had worked around cattle a time before with his pa, working their way to the mining camps . . . He rode a short stocky bay mare, a good horse for working cattle as she could make quick turns . . . Bob wore a tied down Schofield, a gun quick to be reloaded, not as smooth to handle as a Colt, but a very worthy sidearm . . . Wade glanced at it being tied low, "You better know how to use it if you're going to wear it like that, it's an invitation to trouble" . . .

"It's my pa's, he bought it down in Abilene, gave twelve dollars for it, but I know how to use it, I'm pretty quick too" . . .

"Be careful son, there's always some one faster, shooting straight is better than being fast, you might not get a chance with a second shot" . . .

Ted Hooper seemed to not be able to quit talking, he had been going nonstop this morning . . . He rode a gray speckled gelding with a black mane and tail and black feet, Wade always liked good hard black hooves . . . He carried a 51 Navy Colt chambered in a 36 caliber front loader . . . Wade smiled at him, glancing down: "Keep her dry" . . .

John Black wasn't much older than Willy he didn't figure, he rode a sorrel mare, a little thin chested for Wade he thought to himself, looked like a gated horse, John packed an Old Army 44, it was tied to the back of his saddle with his bedroll, Wade figured that was a good place for it too . . .

Letting down the log rails of the opening that lead out into the open prairie and riding through then setting the rails back up, Wade gave each instructions, spreading out to the west and north, they rounded up everything in sight and started moving them to the east, it was a good eight hours of hard riding before they had them all bunched up and headed out . . . Small bunches tried to get back behind and towards the water holes, it was an endless job keeping them bunched up, until they had them out of the valley and well on their way . . .

Wade took Willy and instructed the other three to keep them moving east, Wade and Willy rode back and took a wide berth around the water holes and brushy areas looking for any strays, picking up eleven more head that had been missed, they pushed them hard and got caught up with the rest by dark . . .

An open valley that had a small stream that ran down along one side, the cattle were ready to rest for the night as they spread out down the streams edge, watering . . . With plenty of grass to graze on during the night hours, camp was set up, Wade gave each one a chore to do, from getting wood for the fire to hauling in some water and they would take turns at cooking each night . . .

Willy had shot two jackrabbits and one grouse earlier in the day, they were cleaned and soaked in water ready to be fixed . . .

Wade pulled a small bag of salt and one of pepper and rubbed it into them and fixed two forked sticks and skewered each on green saplings and placed them over the fire about ten inches above the flames, turning them often . . .

It was a good meal and all of them ate their fill . . . After eating, the boys set around the fire asking questions of each other and to see who could tell the biggest lies . . . Many a lifelong friendship were born around an open fire . . .

Wade had saddled his sorrel back up and rode out amongst the cattle, making a wide berth around them pushing them in a tighter circle, he could hear the boys laughing and talking back at the camp . . . Wade set his horse in the dark of the night, thinking of Mary, but something more was nagging at his thoughts . . . Three days before they left for the drive, Wade had been up on the high valley checking cattle, when he picked up tracks from a strange horse, he had followed the tracks which led him to a small campsite of one man, set out of sight and high above the valley amongst the trees, on the west slope, but then tracks of another horse and rider had showed up later, a man wearing flat soled boots . . . There was no one better at reading sign than Wade . . . Wade had taught himself to read sign since he was a young boy, and to this day, would always check his own tracks, when he would ride out of the morning he would check his tracks when he came back in to see how much they had changed in a day, a day with sunshine, a day without sunshine . . . After searching about the camp, he found a couple of places where this man had dug two holes, not big holes, not more than two or three feet wide and deep . . . But had left, Wade had tracked him back over the high ranges that led back west . . . Maybe it was just some one passing through, but it kept creeping back into Wades thoughts . . . What was this man doing in his valley? He mentioned nothing of it to Mary, but had told Ramos to pack his Walker with him when he left the ranch . . . Ramos asked no questions but would do as instructed . . .

Wade rode back into camp and the boys seemed to get quiet, "Don't mind me boys, just remember, the first liar ain't got a chance" . . . Bob Mocker was fooling with his Schofield, pulling it in and out of the holster, Wade thought to himself that this was a boy looking for trouble . . .

Morning rolled in earlier than the boys were ready for, it had been a hard day the day before, and things wouldn't be much better today . . . The sun was just cracking the dawn in the eastern skyline casting it's reddish glow out across the vast prairie, the air was chilly to say the least, fog lifted off the stream that ran past their camp, it left a damp feeling that added to the chill of the air, birds were singing their morning praises . . .

Wade was up and gone, they wondered how he was able to get up and saddled and none of them had heard a noise, the fire was stoked and the coffee pot was hot . . .

Wade rode back into camp: "Let's get em moving fellas, we're burning daylight, Willy you ride point today, get out ahead of them and watch for the best trail, don't bypass any watering holes or good grass, we'll keep em coming your way, Bob and Ted, you take the east side and I'll bring along the west side, John, you clean up camp and catch up shortly, come in on the west side and bring up the rear . . . Let's move em out" . . .

Wade turned reign and went back out to the cattle, the four of them looked at each other and then quickly scrambled to their feet, packing up bedrolls and picking up a few pieces of jerky Wade had left laying on a rock next to the coffee pot, Willy was the first saddled and headed out towards Wade with a shout, his roan gelding kicking up the dust as they sped down into the open prairie . . . Ted and Bob weren't far behind and they started the cattle moving on east . . . John cleaned up camp and tossed the round of rocks back into the brush and wiped away their tracks as Wade had instructed them to do . . . He flung his leg up over his horse and off they flew, he had caught up in a matter of minutes . . .

The cattle moved out much easier this morning as they were in unfamiliar grounds and moving east towards fresh grass seemed like the right thing to do, keeping in the strays on the sides was easier today, there was not much brush or trees here, so they let them fan out to a wider group taking in as much grazing as they could . . .

Willy came riding back into the herd informing Wade of a huge herd of buffalo to the west, so they pushed the west side of cattle back in and farther to the east, buffalo and cattle didn't mix well out in the open prairies and the cattle would spook and scatter too easily . . .

The farther east they pushed, the scarcer the water and grass became and more restless the cattle were at night . . . They would take shifts during the night, riding around the herd keeping them bunched in a tighter circle to avoid having to round them up from such a wide group each morning, saving hours of time and work . . .

Each night around the fire Bob would pull out his Schofield and handle it. Slide it in and out of the holster . . . Wade would check his holster each night as well but it would always be when on his watch when no one was aware, he checked it for dirt and function each night . . . Bob had questioned Wade at times of his speed of draw . . . Bob had drew quickly a couple of times to show Wade just how fast he was . . . Wade would always put him off: "Don't go there son, a gunslinger lives a short life, a lonely life, a life of looking over your shoulder" . . .

This night was different, Bob had pushed it farther, annoying Wade . . . Wade knew this kid needed a lesson, a lesson now, one that would leave him still alive . . . Wade had grown fond of the four of these kids . . .

"Wade stood up: "So you want to see how fast you are do you? Do you want to draw on me?"

"Oh no sir Mr. Tavner, but don't you think I'm good?"

"It's one thing to be fast Bob, but you got to shoot straight as well, and your target just might be shooting back at you" . . .

"Well I can shoot straight, my pa taught me that," as Bob continued to goad the issue . . .

Wade picked up two rocks about as big around as a man's fist and walked about thirty paces and placed them on top of a dead tree limb about waist high, "Lets just see how good and fast you are then Bob" . . . He then handed John his coffee cup, "Stand behind us John where neither one of us can see you, toss my coffee cup in the air, now Bob, when that cup hits the ground you see if you can shoot your rock before I do mine" . . .

Bob was all smiles, he was sure he could beat Wade . . .

"You ready Bob?"

"Yes sir, I'm ready" as his hand twitched nervously, hovering just over the grip of his Schofield . . .

"Ok John, you toss the cup anytime you feel like it" . . .

John waited a second or two, and then tossed the cup as far up as he could, he wanted to see the outcome of this . . . The cup hit the ground with a tinny sound as it landed on the rocky ground, Bob's hand hit the grip on his Schofield as quickly as he could muster, but before the barrel cleared leather, Wades colt had fired twice and shattered not only the rock on the left but the one on the right as well and had holstered his gun before Bob got his Schofield leveled off . . .

Wade quietly pulled his colt back out and ejected the spent shells and replaced them with new ones from his belt, then looked at Bob still standing in amazement, "Good thing we weren't shooting at each other huh? Remember this Bob, there is always some one faster than you or me, and then there are those who would just as soon shoot you in the back as well" . . .

Willy was laughing so hard he fell plum to the ground rolling in the dirt . . . John walked up and slapped Bob on the back, "Try him again Bob, I thought you about had him, maybe you'll get him this time," as he broke into a full bellied laugh of his own . . .

Ted, leaning on a mesquite limb, "Wooooooooweeeeeeeeeee Bob, you'd be looking up at the sky through a pile of rocks" . . .

Bob swallowed hard as there was an extra lump of pride in his throat . . . Later in the evening as Wade took his turn at night watch, the four of them hashed out the speed of Wades gun, and they all badgered Bob whether he wanted to try again . . .

Setting his horse amongst the cows, Wade thought to himself that he hoped the little endeavor would make Bob think real hard about pulling his gun on a man, then his thoughts returned to Mary and Three Valley Ranch and Ramos and Roscoe . . . He missed them all . . .

Morning had rolled in with the sound of distant thunder and clouds looming over camp, it left a damp feeling in the air and the fire felt good as it can get cold out in the high prairies in the darkness of night, Wade rode into camp as they were packing up: "You better leave your slickers out boys, it's going to be a wet day today" . . .

By noon it was a steady rain, nothing hard, but a rain that soaks you to the bone and everything you're carrying . . . Riding, pushing cattle as the dreary day hung on, collars pulled up around their necks, heads hunkered down, rain running from the brim of their hats . . . Dark settled in an hour or two earlier tonight, the rain subsided to a drizzle, camp was a muddy mess, a fire hard to kindle, but hot coffee seemed to taste better than any cup they had ever had, throwing the bedrolls down was a question of mud or rock . . .

Wade smiling at them: "It's a good life ain't it boys?" as he pulled inside his bedroll and it seemed he fell asleep within minutes . . .

Ted Hooper thought to himself, he didn't know if this would be worth thirty dollars a month or not . . .

They had reached the Platte River by the end of the month, turning the herd south towards the rail head, water would be a plenty now and the cows could be crowded against the river the rest of the way . . . Reaching the railways in nearly five weeks of driving, the cattle looked good as they had good green grass all the way here . . .

At the rail yards, corrals had been built to hold the cattle drives that were coming up from Texas, and there were a thousand head in the corrals at the time, But the cattle being driven from Texas had much harsher conditions and very little grass coming up across the plain states of the mid west, and these cattle were bone thin . . . Wades cattle were slick and fat . . . They had arrived two days ahead of the cattle auction . . .

The auctions started at 8:00 AM sharp, and the cattle from Texas would be auctioned off first as they had arrived in that order, with the bulk of the lot bringing thirteen dollars a head, a little short of what Wade was hoping for, he had planned on seventeen to eighteen and was planning on paying off the note against their ranch with the money, the note held over his ranch did not set easy with Wade . . .

The bidding started on Wades cattle with the five of them setting on the top rail of the divided corrals, the bidding started at nine dollars a head but quickly shot to fourteen and slowed but kept a steady pace to nineteen fifty . . . It was more than Wade had expected, the boys watching, felt as excited about it as Wade himself, after all, it was their herd to bring in . . .

Wade received his check and the five of them headed into town . . . Wade stopped in at the bank and cashed his check, it was more than enough to pay off the note on their ranch . . . He paid his four hands thirty dollars each: "I got thirty more for you when we get back home, I don't want you boys losing all of your money here, I heard you fellas talking that you want to stay in town a few days, and I don't blame you one bit, you've earned it, I would myself if I was you, Myself, well I am heading back just as soon as I can fetch my horse, there's several hours of daylight left and I plan to make the best of them . . . Remember boys, don't touch a man's hat, or thieve his horse, or get caught looking at his woman" . . .

John Black had an uncle living on the outskirts of Denver, the four of them decided to stay for a few days and see the town and live it up a spell before heading back home, Bob wasn't even sure he was going to head back to Silver Creek Springs . . .

Wade bode them a farewell and a good time: "I got the rest of your pay when you get there, it will be waiting for you, Bob, keep that Schofield in the holster" . . .

"Not a problem there sir" . . .

Wade stashed the remainder of the money in his saddlebags and stepped into the saddle with much eagerness to get back home, he reigned the big sorrel north out past the cattle corrals and gave him his head and the big sorrel picked a good pace, He had two days of rest and he seemed anxious to get back as well . . . Covering the ground as old times would have . . . Crossing the Platte, Wade turned into the mountainous regions to take the shortest route back, he figured he could shave off a couple of days riding, he was anxious to see Mary . . .

Wade thought to himself that if he were home tonight it wouldn't be soon enough . . .

Chapter 12

Wade had pushed the big sorrel well into the late afternoon hours, with nothing on his mind but getting home as soon as he could get there . . . They had just topped out on top of the lower ranges when the sorrel jerked his head to the left, ears erect, Wade had just caught the flash of sunlight on something about the same time, Wade quickly pulled the reigns to turn him sharply to the right, but it was a second to late, the flash of gun muzzle and the echoing boom that followed hit home, Wade could feel the sorrel going down under him, blood was splattered on his face and shirt, as he barreled off his horse sliding the Winchester from the scabbard as he went, and dove into a depression in the ground just a few feet of where his horse had went down, hearing the zing of bullets whizzing by as he landed belly down on the ground with a thud . . .

Wade lift his head slightly to see if he could see who was out there, "SPLAT" a bullet rips into the dirt and shatters against a rock that sends fragments of debris that stings against the side of his face and ear . . . Wade swore . . .

Wades sorrel lay thrashing on the ground not more than ten feet from him, he could see he'd been shot through the neck just above the withers, a bullet intended for him no doubt, his horse was in pain and squealing trying to gain his feet, Wade could tell he was done, his neck bone had been shattered by the bullet, so he pulled his Winchester to his shoulder and squeezed the trigger, putting his horse out of pain and misery . . .

An anger grew strong within himself, first for letting himself ride into an ambush as this, he should have seen some sign, tracks or anything, he had three years worth of money, they had worked hard for in his saddle bags, still strapped to his horse, money they needed to pay the note on their ranch, and if not paid they could possibly loose the ranch, his mind had been on nothing but getting back to see Mary, and for having to shoot his own horse, one of the best horses he'd ever owned . . . He thought to himself, he should have known better . . .

There was not more than two hours of daylight left and he knew he would really be in trouble then as they could slip around and surround him and pick him off, he knew he had to get out of this hole, he lay there surveying everything around him, this looked like an old volcano dome with lava rock lined around the rim which was no more that fifteen feet wide and sunken down a good three feet . . .

They would occasionally fire rounds into the surrounding rocks, keeping Wade pinned down . . .

Over to Wades right lay his horse, in front of him were men shooting at him, behind him was too open and running straight away left to easy a shot, to his left were some small pines and large rocks littered around with heavy forest of pines beyond that . . . Wade lay there listening to the shots fired, most all guns have a distinct sound, different than others, Wade thought he could count four different guns, Wade could also hear them talking amongst themselves, occasionally one was laughing, making Wade even madder that they would think he was just going to let them have it this easy . . .

Wade crawled to the far right side, getting to his horse would be death for sure, he would have to leave the saddle bags with the money, saving his life was more than risking that, at the far right side of the depression he was laying in stood a short sapling of a pine, not more than an inch in diameter but stood a good four feet high, Wade reached up a little but keeping his hand below the rim of his hole and slowly pulled the pine over to the ground, pulling it as slow as he could so as not to draw anyone's attention to it, it felt like ten minutes had passed, they had not fired any shots for several minutes and things seemed too quiet, once he got the sapling pulled to the ground he lay a rock on the top limbs, a rock just big enough to hold it down, then he wedged his hat on the top limbs, then crawled to the far left rim, grabbing his Winchester in his left hand and tossing a rock towards the rock that held the pine down he dislodged it and up sprang the pine and into the air towards his horse went his hat, guns boomed, at the same instant Wade jumped from his cover and raced towards the rocks and trees, it was enough distraction that he made it to the cover he intended for, bullets seemed to whiz by as he hit the darkness of the trees, he could at least move about, he could shoot back now as well . . . Wade had a clear view of his horse from here, although he couldn't see them . . .

The four men cursed at each other now, wishing they had got him with that first shot, now he was loose and ready to fight back . . . This was suppose to be an easy task . . .

Wade set patiently; he could see if they made a move towards him or the saddlebags, and it wasn't but a few minutes until one of them made a run towards his horse, Wade leveled his Winchester and laid the sights on the man and squeezed the trigger, he made one loud yell and humped up and fell face first into the dirt just short of Wades sorrel . . . Shots rang out in the direction of where Wade had fired, but Wade had already moved positions not giving them a chance at a lucky shot . . .

Wade was hunkered down under a spruce, a spruce with heavy limbs that reached all the way down to the ground, with other pines thickly spaced about, he was completely hid from sight . . . He could hear them talking and was sure that there were only three of them left, one of them wanted to get the money and light out, the bigger and older looking man said: "We've been paid to do a job and we'll get the money when the job's done" . . .

They had spread out and working their way towards where Wade lay in wait, dodging from rock to rock, yelling back and forth if anyone has seen him or any sign, the younger one hollers back: "I think maybe one of us got him when he was running into the trees, let's get the money and get out of here" . . .

The bigger man is obvious the one in charge here and Wade sees him quietly stepping through the woods from tree to tree, the man is standing behind a tree peering out into where he last saw Wade, thinking Wade was ahead of him, but he is directly to his right now . . . Wade levels off his rifle and takes a dead aim, the bullet splatters bark and enters through the man's right lung and out his left, gasping for a breath, he fires his gun into the ground twice before he falls to the ground coughing out blood as he drops . . . Wade lay motionless under his thick cover . . .

One of the two left hollers at his partner: "Sam, this ain't worth dying for, let's get out of here now" . . . Wade couldn't see them, but could hear foot steps running back to their horses . . .

After a few minutes, Wade crawls from under the spruce and walks towards the man he just shot, rolls him over and looks at him, a face that looked familiar maybe, but he couldn't place where, he'd seen a lot of faces over the past years, he digs through the man's pockets, but nothing there to tell who he was . . . Wade walked back to his horse and pulls the saddlebags off and un-cinches his saddle and pulls it out from under his sorrel . . . There lies the other man he shot earlier, and rolls him over, and takes a good look, this man he knew he had seen in Silver Creek Springs lately and starts to wonder, if this was just a coincidence or had they came to kill him or rob him, or both . . . .

Dark had set in now, a cup of coffee sounded good, but he felt he dared not build a fire, he carried his saddle a good quarter a mile from his horse and laid it down and spread out his bedroll and took out a piece of jerky he'd picked up just before heading out . . . Wade's ears were now tuned to every sound of the night, sleep would be hard if any, but he was tired and his eyes drifted off . . .

It was still dark of the night when a noise awoke him, every sense of his being was wide awake and full bore, adrenaline racing in his veins, his ears tuned for any sound not normal to the night, his eyes were focused to the dark, the colt that lay next to him in the bedroll was instantly in his hand, and again, a limb snapped not more than a hundred feet away, squinting into the darkness of the trees he saw movement, a shadow cast by the dim glow of less than a half moon, Wade was absolutely motionless, the shadow stepped out from the trees and what little moonlight there was revealed one of the dead men's horse, Wade standing to his feet talked softly to the horse and moved towards him in a slow deliberate fashion, reaching out and taking the reigns which hung to the ground, unsaddling him and pulling some grass and rubbing his back down, removing the bit from his mouth and fashioning a halter from his lariat and tying him off in some green grass . . .

Wade could hardly wait till daylight to get on his way home, but first he went and found the tracks of the two that rode off yesterday, their tracks led due west and he planned on heading northwest, but he would follow their tracks for a ways to be sure they weren't going to double back on him . . . One of the horses must have had a split hoof, for the front left shoe had a forged bar across the toe, something a blacksmith would do for a remedy of a bad hoof . . .

It was still several days ride and the sooner he got started the sooner he would be able to surprise Mary, He would be home a good week or two sooner than they had thought . . .

Saddling up the chestnut mare he gave her a good look over, not a horse he would choose for his own mount, thin in the chest and feet to close together, a skinny neck and small withers, but she would do for now . . . He swung into the saddle and almost smiled, she was short coupled compared to his sorrel, he could reach out and touch her ears, her stride was smooth but not near as long, this horse wouldn't have near the stamina he was used to either . . . He pushed her as hard as he thought he could, he figured he could have covered a few more miles a day with his own mount . . .

Wade had pushed the little chestnut mare for seven straight days when he topped the range that led down into their valley, he couldn't wait to clear that next ridge, he would be able to see the cabin from there, he spurred her into a faster pace with so much eagerness to be home and see Mary . . .

They topped the last ridge and were not more than a quarter mile from the cabin as it came into view, Wades smile quickly faded . . . Something was not right, he could see that the corral gate was open and the horses were out and gone, he could see no life around the house, but then Mary and Ramos could be out checking cattle at this time of day, it was a cool damp day, Wade wore his jacket, but there was no smoke from the chimney . . . Wades instincts, he pulled the Winchester and rode easily down to the cabin, taking in everything around the place, nothing moved, but so many things seemed wrong, the water bucket at the front door was lying on it's side, the corral being empty, even if they were checking cows, there should be three other horses in there, looking down, Wade quickly spotted tracks of strange horses, tying off the little chestnut mare he studied the tracks, they were a few days old, maybe even a week, four riders had come in from the west side of the valley, not the normal route anyone would use, Wade could see tracks of one man walking to the right side of the cabin and he followed them, they led into the short brush between the cabin and the river, Wade stepped through the brush and found Ramos lying there, face down, he was dead, he'd been shot in the back, three times, tracks showed whoever shot him stood behind him and shot him three times deliberately in the back, Ramos' old walker lay beside him, unfired . . .

Wade heard movement towards the front of the cabin, a scuffle type of noise, then it quit, He quickly worked his way around in front, his colt drawn, hammer cocked and finger on the trigger, he stood quietly, listening to every sound, and then he heard the noise again, it was under the front porch of the cabin, Wade got down on his knees and about the same time, Roscoe crawled from under the porch, he had been shot twice, once through the right front shoulder and once through his left hind quarter, his golden colored hair was soaked with dried blood . . . Wade picked him up and laid him on an ole rug laying on the porch and ran to the creek with the water bucket and cleaned his wounds . . . He didn't know how he was still alive . . . He stroked his big head: "Where's Mary big fella?" . . . The big dog just lay there looking up at Wade through those big brown eyes, eyes of sadness . . .

Dark had settled in, Wade couldn't read any more sign until day light arrived, it would be a long night . . . Wade had never felt anger like this before, his blood seemed to boil within . . .

Wade was up well before daylight, he had gotten Roscoe to eat some dried biscuits soaked with bacon grease, one of his favorites, he had moved the big dog inside close to the fire, Roscoe had drank some water, probably the first water he'd had all week, he could barely crawl . . .

As soon as it was light enough to see, Wade was out trying to decipher the sign of what had happened, four horses had rode in, but five had rode out, and one of them was Mary's black, he knew that because Wade had always marked the shoes of his own horses, when he shod his horses, he always put one slash mark angled across the inside heel of the front left shoe on his horse and put two slashes on Mary's, she didn't even know he did this, Wade could always tell their tracks from anyone else . . .

So he was sure she was alive, at least she was when she left, she hadn't left willingly as you could see where there had been a scuffle getting her on her horse, she had been knocked down once, as her knees and handprints were on the ground in the dust, and it was the same tracks by Ramos that had shot him in the back, by the depth of the tracks compared to the rest, he was a big man, a man of a good two hundred and fifty pounds or more . . . The tracks led to the west, towards Silver Creek Springs . . .

The big long legged palomino stood out in the valley, Wade whistled for him and he came into the corral for a handout of oats, shutting the gate behind him, Wade was glad to have him to ride over the chestnut mare. He turned her out into the valley to graze . . . He picked up Roscoe and carried him into the barn and lay him on a bed of hay, brought him plenty of food for several days and two buckets of water, then stroked the big fellas head and told him sorry, but he had to go find Mary . . .

He saddled up the big horse and took a wide sweep around the cabin, reading sign, only the tracks of the four riders were found, but not being satisfied with that, Wade took a bigger loop farther out checking for any sign, sure enough, on that pass, he ran across the tracks of another horseman, he followed them to the ridge that overlooked the cabin from above, one of the only places you could see the cabin and what was going on, the man dismounted and watched everything from here it appeared, the man smoked rolled tobacco and wore flat soled boots, and he left heading west also, towards Silver Creek Springs . . .

Wade tracked them at a fast pace as they seemed to have no worries and made no attempt to cover their tracks at all . . . But before they got within a mile or two of Silver Creek Springs they held up shortly and one of them rode into town and Wade followed his track into town, but the tracks led into the livery and that could have been any number of a hundred people going and coming on any given day . . .

Wade had brought the saddlebag of money with him, pulling it from his horse he stepped into the bank . . . Walking up to the tellers window he opens the bags and draws out the money and hands it to the teller, "I want to pay off the note on our ranch and put thirty dollars each in an account for Willy Stone, Bob Mocker, Ted Hooper and John Black and then put what's left in our ranch account" . . .

The teller looks at him with astonishment . . .

Wade scowls down at him as he doesn't have time, "Something you don't understand here?"

"Uh no sir, but I had heard Mr. Simmons say that he had gotten a telegram stating that you had been shot and killed on your way from Denver" . . .

With anger looming in his voice: "I don't look dead do I ? What else you hear? What have you heard about Mary?"

The little teller seems reluctant to say anymore . . .

Wade pulls the colt from the holster and grabs him by the collar of his shirt and pulls his face right into the bars of the booth and puts the barrel of the colt under his chin, "I won't ask again what do you know about Mary!"

"Well sir, the word is that she went back east to her family, she had no need of a ranch on her own out here, and Mr. Simmons had foreclosed on your ranch" . . .

If Wade wasn't already angry enough, "Foreclosed!! I got two more months left on that note, he can't foreclose it, get the paperwork out now, You write paid in full on it and sign it and give me a copy as well" . . .

"Why I can't sign those papers, only Mr. Simmons can"...

"You'll sign them or I'll sign them with your blood splattered on them, where is Mr. Simmons anyway, I got a few words for him as well"...

"He is back east, he took the stage out of town last week to attend a bankers convention and seminar"...

Wade glancing over at his desk noticed a rolled tobacco lying in an ashtray on his desk...

Wade took his copy of the papers and folded them up and stashed them away in the saddlebags then stepped into the saddle and headed south to pick up the trail of the men who took Mary... Vengeance was on his mind...

He rode no more than a couple of miles until he picked up the tracks; they turned and headed more in a southwest direction, with the same four riders and Mary, that fifth rider had stayed from their sight and was probably still in Silver Creek Springs, but Wade had no time to try to find who that was...

Only a few miles of tracking led to the camp sight of their first night, Wade took his time checking every detail of their camp, Mary's hands were tied, they were tied over her head at night, He could see the scuff marks around the trunk of a small tree where the rope had rubbed the bark off, he could see where she had laid, he could also see where the same big man had stood at her feet for some time, probably staring at her in the night, he had squatted there, he could tell as when a man squats he leaves no heel prints in the dirt... The fire was out in the open, they had tried to hide nothing, it suddenly dawned on him, they thought he was dead, this was not just a coincidence, these men who had taken Mary were assuming he was dead... They had no fear of him tracking them... This would be a big advantage to him...

Dark was easing it's way into the evening hours, but Wade pushed on into the dark, they were riding in a straight line, Wade had picked a distant landmark for which the tracks were heading and kept a strong pace on the palomino gelding, it was more than likely going on midnight when Wade pulled into a clump of mesquite brush and pulled the saddle from his big horse, there was plenty of water and green grass here, he picketed him close to the water and made sure he had ample grass and brushed his gelding down before he fixed his own morsel of a supper, he was tired, dead tired, but sleep would be little and hard to come by... The moon was not more than half full, but the sky was clear as crystal, allowing the temperatures to drop quickly into the night, a fire would have felt good, but he feared he not risk it... Wade worried if Mary even had a riding jacket along, she would be cold sleeping on the ground, the stars twinkled into the night as Wade felt he had seen everyone of them...

The morning rolled into dawn and the skies lightened up, Wade kindled a small fire, a fire of dead limbs that hardly made any smoke at all, and he built it under an over hanging mesquite bush allowing what little smoke there was to dissipate into the branches, just enough fire to warm a cup of coffee which he tossed in two fingers worth of coffee grounds, the coffee tasted good and felt good to his bones, he took the last bite of his sourdough biscuit and sipped in the last swallow of coffee and swirled it around in his mouth before swallowing it, then tossed the grounds into the dusty ground, putting out what remained of his fire and kicking soft dirt over what ashes were left . . . Cleaning the back of the palomino and tossing the saddle blanket on and then the saddle, checking the bit and headstall and swung into the saddle and proceeded to pick up the trail . . .

After a few hours of tracking he found their second campsite and searched it high and low for any sign that might tell him who they were or where they were headed . . . He thought of Mary, if these men thought he was dead, surely they had told her as well, she would have no hope . . .

Wade had pushed hard, covering a lot more ground than they had, but they had several days head start on him, maybe even a week, he thought maybe he had gained two days on them, he pushed on into the darkness each night . . .

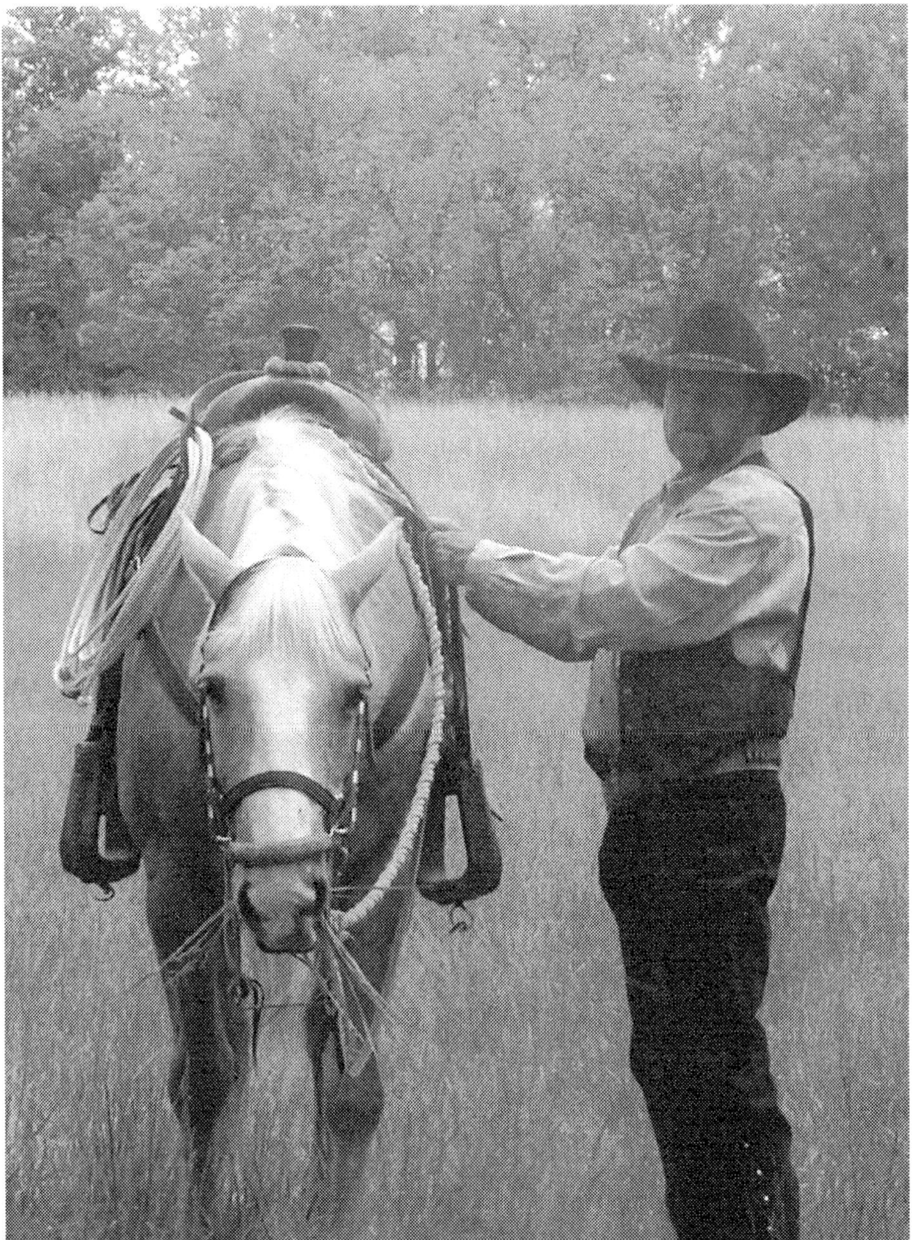

Chapter 13

    A good three days ahead of Wade, Mary Franks lie in her bedroll, her heart ached from her dismal situation, was Wade really dead, they had told her he had been killed, and the big Mexican had laughed about it, and why would she not believe him, she had seen this man shoot Ramos in the back and had shot her dog as well, as Roscoe had attacked them and bit them after slapping her to the ground, this big man was ruthless, the likes she had never seen before . . .
    The sun was setting out across the prairie that lie ahead of them, her heart remembered the days of seeing Wade ride in across their ranch of the evening with the sun setting behind him, thinking that was the most perfect scene her eyes had ever witnessed, Mary's heart ached, tears welled within her eyes, she wished to just die . . .
    She would pretend to be asleep at night as the big Mexican would stand at the foot of where she lie and stare at her during the night, he would often squat and watch her for long periods of time, he was repulsive to her, he was a big man, dirty from head to toe, his hair hung from under the back of his hat and looked as if it hadn't been washed in months, it was oily and dirty, his teeth were yellow from filth, he smelled as a goat to her, he had slid his hand down her arm a time or two and it seemed to make her want to vomit . . . She had learned that his name was Carlos, he had a much longer name, but went by Carlos . . .
    Mary had not a clue to where they were taking her, she figured originally they would take her far from town and just kill her, but it seemed they must be taking her somewhere for a particular reason, but a reason unknown to her, and none of them would tell her nothing . . .

They had been on the trail now for four days, they had stopped for the evening and set up camp . . . Two men on horses rode into camp late, well after dark, their horses worn out, as if they had traveled far and hard, Carlos met them and argued for some time with them, suddenly Mary's ears seemed to pick up as she heard the words of Carlos, "What do you mean you didn't get him?"

The younger of the two spoke up: "Will missed him, he couldn't wait for him to get a little closer, he was afraid he would spot us and hell, he hit his horse and he got under cover and hell Carlos, he killed Will and Spader, we were lucky to get out with our lives" . . . .

Carlos back handed him and knocked him to the ground: "I ought to kill the both of you right now myself, I send you to do an easy task and you can't even ambush a man, why did you let Will shoot him?"

"You know Will was a friend of Billy, he wanted to be the one who pulled the trigger on him" . . .

"Well where's the money?"

"Carlos, we didn't get that either, Spader made a run for it and he shot him dead in his tracks" . . .

"What? You didn't even get the loot? Now you know he's trailing us out there right now, we got his woman, the man will be wanting death on his hands, our death . . . Come first light, you two are going to lay wait for him, and you better be sure he is dead this time, you understand that, or there won't be another time for you two, I will personally see to that" . . .

Mary's heart had a glimmer of hope, had she heard right, were they even talking about Wade, surely they were, or was it just her imagination of hope, but whatever, it was hope . . .

Carlos handed her a plate, brown beans with salted pork fat, Mary smiles at him, "He will catch us you know, and he will end your miserable life" . . .

In a fit of rage, Carlos slapped the plate from her hands, scattering the beans on anyone standing within twenty feet: "He will not be so lucky this time, his life will end very soon, we will be in Purgatory Wells in two days and then it will be too late for you too señorita, you will bring a fancy price, maybe I will have my way with you before we get there and for sure after then, maybe I will be the best thing in line waiting for a chance with you, you see it will not be so easy a life for you there, but you will not have a choice, and no one there will care what you like or don't like" . . .

Mary's heart was nearly to pound out of her chest, she could feel it pounding in her throat, she could feel sweat beading on her forehead, she had never felt an anger like this before, she scraped the toe of her boot in the loose dirt and kicked it in his face . . .

He reached down and back hands her across her face, splitting her lip with the back of his big knuckles, he grabbed her by the front of her jacket and lifts her off the ground as if she weighed nothing . . .

One of the other men pulls a gun and levers a shell into the chamber, "Leave her be Carlos, she won't be worth nothing to us if she's dead or beat up" . . .

He drops her back to the ground, Mary unable to get her feet under her, landing back against the trunk of a tree hitting with a thud, nearly knocking the wind out of her . . .

Carlos gave her a look of hatred: "I will enjoy my time with you" . . . then focused his attention to the man holding the Winchester on him: "You better never pull a gun on me again Buck, if you do, you better pull the trigger quick or I'll use it on you" . . .

Night settled in quickly and the dark overtook the evening, there was a coldness in the air, not only from the night chill, but a coldness of the camp . . .

Mary's heart had a glimmer of hope, she knew Wade was still alive, but she also knew they would be waiting for him, and planned to set a trap and kill him, she also knew they were taking her to Purgatory Wells, she had never heard of the place, maybe she would find help there . . .

Mary lie in her bedroll awake, waiting for everyone to fall asleep, she listened and watched, she could hear each man's breath, only when she knew they were all asleep, she pulled herself up close to the tree which her hands were tied around, a small tree no more than four inches in diameter at the base, there was a small bush on the other side that hung over against the tree, she moved slowly and quietly, getting some slack in the rope, reaching under the bush on the other side, she scrolled in the dirt with her finger, PURGATORY WELLS . . .

Chapter 14

Wade knew he had gained ground on them, the last camp still had some warmth in the ground under the pit of ashes, but there had been some big logs thrown on during the night that could have burned for several hours, and they didn't appear to do anything about cleaning up a camp and doing away with a fire, whatever ashes were going were just left . . . They might still be two to three days ahead of him, he feared something would happen to Mary before he caught them, either way, he would continue tracking them and do what justice needed to be done . . . They had stayed well clear of any towns, towns were few and far between out here anyway, but they knew two things that would get you in more trouble, that were not tolerated in the west, and that was horse thieving and mistreating a woman, especially a woman with the looks of Mary, a rarity out here . . .

Their tracks had led more to the west in the last day, this was a tough hard country they were heading into, a barren land, a wasteland to any who had seen it, a land without much water if any during the summer months, a land Wade had rarely traveled, he had set around many a campfire listening to the stories of those who had traveled in other parts of this country, he shared camps with a Calvary scout, an apache, one who had traveled here many times, Wade tried to remember the things he had told him of this area and of what things to look for . . . Wade was a good listener, knowing that even the wildest of stories has some thread of truth in them . . .

Wade pulled up reign on his gelding, stepping down from the saddle, he saw new tracks, they had come in from the east, riding hard, the horses appeared to be worn out as they were dragging the toes of their feet and not placing the rear foot in the depression of the front foot . . .

Wade spits into the dirt and looks up at his big horse: "Shit, big fella, things just made a big change in the plans", he bends down and rubs his hand across the tracks, "This here horse got a forged bar across his front left shoe, seems like we ain't got no luck at all boy, they're going to be watching for us now" . . .

It's open country for another good mile ahead of them and these boys hadn't caught up with them yet, so they wouldn't be looking for him yet, so Wade kept the pace brisk to as far out as he could see, riding into a clump of cottonwoods, Wade finds their camp, and can tell that the other two riders showed up, the camp was cold now, the fire had been put out, Wade wandered around, he could tell where all had been bedded down, he squatted down and looked at everything as he always did, looking for any sign or clue, he found the tree where he could tell Mary had been tied, and just as he was about to stand up and walk away, he caught a glimpse of something out of normal, just on the other side of the tree was a wild rose bush, a small piece of material was slightly flickering in the light breeze under the bush, he squats back down and pushes the limbs back, a two inch piece of Mary's sleeve was dangling, tied to one of the under branches, and scratched in the ground, PURGATORY WELLS . . .

Wade swore bitterly, he had heard of the place, it was a place fitting to it's name, a small town of Mexican thieves and bandits, there wasn't a decent person in this town, it had started as nothing more than a hideout and had attracted every low life living in the country, it was a lawless place, it set on the west edge of Devils Gulch, or some called it the Den of Satin or the Devils Lair, a valley that was told to be not crossable from the east . . . Their tracks had turned northward, Wade knew they would have to travel northward to get around the north end of this wasteland, a good two to three days ride on a good horse, but he also remembered the apache scout telling him that he had crossed the Valley of Satin twice, Wade had questioned him at the time, and he believed he had actually crossed it . . . Wade asked him what he would have done if his horse couldn't make it, and was told he would eat his horse and walk across it, and the both had laughed, but Wade knew he probably wasn't lying about that fact either . . . Wade drew back on his memories of his conversations with him, and the apache had told him he had entered at Twin Sisters Rocks . . .

This would be an awful risky gamble for Wade to take, but it might be the only chance he had of catching them before they got to Purgatory Wells, and if they made it there, well a thought he couldn't let himself consider, and he also knew that they would be laying in wait with an ambush for him now too, and that he might not be as lucky this time . . .

Wade pulled reign on the palomino and headed due south, opposite the direction they had taken, along the eastern edge of this huge barren wasteland, the sun was high and the heat waves danced across the horizon, blocking all sign of the distant sea of prairie, riding for nearly five hours along the east rim finding only one small watering hole from which he filled his canteen and let his gelding get his fill, seeing nothing that he would consider Twin Sisters Rocks, had he made a wrong decision to take this route, had the apache told an untruth, would he never see Mary Franks again . . . It would be dark soon and Wade needed to stop and rest the big horse, but something loomed in the evening horizon not more than a quarter mile ahead of him so he pushed on a little farther, riding up to what his eyes had spotted a ways back, stood two lava rocks, not more than five feet tall, spread about fifteen feet apart, this had to be what the apache called Twin Sisters Rocks, also in the area were some short cactus scattered about and some chewed off buffalo grass, looking the area over he found some antelope tracks leading around behind the farther rock . . . Wade could see there had been water here at one time, the ground still seemed damp . . . He found a small flat rock and dug into the ground creating a hole a good fifteen inches deep, the ground would pack into a ball, there was some moisture in it . . . He had tied his horse off close to the canyon amongst the short grass, he stripped him of his saddle and pad and removed the headstall, then kindled a small fire and pulled out a piece of jerky from his saddle bags, he emptied what little was left in his canteen into the cup and boiled a cup of coffee, he was dead tired, he had put in long hours in the saddle, and mentally he felt exhausted . . .

Morning rolled around it seemed in minutes, as his body fell sound asleep for the first night in a long time, the sun would be up soon and he could check out his surroundings and see if there was a passage down into the valley below . . . Wade walked over to the far rock where he had dug his hole, and sure enough, it was half full of water, the hole was below ground level and what water was in the soil had leached into the hole, he filled his canteen and took a few swallows, it tasted salty from the alkali soil, but it was cool from the evening air, he then went and got his gelding and brought him to drink, there was not more than a gallon or two of water in the hole, but as the gelding drank it down to within an inch of the bottom, it trickled in more . . .

While the big horse drank and pulled at the short grass there by the water, Wade wandered over to the sharp drop off that entered into the valley below, it dropped off more than a hundred feet straight down it seemed, almost feeling scary to stand too close to the edge fearing it could cave off . . . Looking farther south, Wade could see a thin thread of a trail, angling downward to the bottom, walking down to it, the trail was not more than two feet wide at any given point, he could see no sign that anyone or anything had been down the trail for a long time, it angled down and around the next bend and you couldn't see if it made it all the way down to the bottom, and if a person started down this on horse and the trail played out or had fallen away, there would be no way of turning around, it would be death . . .

Wade had took the gamble to come this way, to chance a shortcut, and he had to take the gamble further, it didn't matter either way, it wasn't a choice now, he had to do it . . .

Saddled back up he started the gelding down the thin trail, balking at first at the sight of the sheer drop off, any misplaced footing here and they would both be remains at the bottom, with a little coaxing and reassurance from Wade he stepped onto it and headed down, Wade gave him the lead with slack reigns, "You take it at your pace big fella" . . . Wade's left knee and shoulder scraped against the side in several places as they passed on down into the Devils Lair, rounding the bend, Wade could see the trail leading all the way to the bottom, and let out a sigh of relief, the farther down they went it seemed the hotter it grew, Wade felt it was like looking into a hot fire, there was a breeze lifting up from the canyon floor, but it was hot, it seemed to take your breath away . . .

    Once down on the valley floor they headed due west, you couldn't see the far side, heat waves danced across the valley floor and dust lifted from each footstep, a grayish white powdery dust that seemed to find it's way to your nostrils and eyes . . . By mid day the sun was oppressive, Wade had stopped and took a small swallow of water from his canteen, then taking his bandana and wet it thoroughly and cleaned the nostrils and mouth of his horse as the dust had caked to it, he felt like he needed to cough and wheeze as well, he wrapped the wetted bandana around his neck, there was no relief from the heat, there was no shade or water, nothing to break the extreme heat, he wondered to himself, what have I done, we may both die down here . . .

    Leading his horse they plodded on and still couldn't see the west rim, the sun had reached the western sky though and was dropping down into the distant horizon, they would go from extreme heat to a cold night, it was amazing how hot the desert could be in the heat of the sun and how cold it could drop at night . . . They had seen no sign of life, nary a rabbit or even a horned toad, nothing . . .

    Wade spotted a knoll not far from them, the heat waves had eased and he headed towards it, it stood no more than five feet, Wade stepped up on it and swore he could see an outcropping of rocks not far to the north and some scattered cactus about, but also realized that a man's imagination plays tricks on him at these odds . . . Once the sun dropped it would be dark in no time here, they pressed on towards the area he swore was rocks and cactus . . . Sure enough it was, and at one time had contained water, a small spring time spring, but it was powdery dry now . . . He took another swallow of water and washed the nostrils of his horse again, the big horse needed water, Wade knew a lot of horses that couldn't have endured this at all, that would have already dropped, this horse had the stamina and endurance of any he'd ever known . . .

    Wade pulled the saddle from his back and rubbed him down and cleaned him off of the dust, removing his own hat and knocking the dust from it as well as his own clothes . . . Taking his bowie from the back of his belt, it was a big knife, a survival type knife, with a heavy strong spine and a brass hilt, with walnut handles, Wade always kept it sharp, with the weight of it, a good swing could cut through a two inch spruce limb, it was sharpened to a point as well, he had used it for a hammer as well as cutting up a deer, he took the bowie and walked over to one of the barrel cactus and cut off the top one third of it then carved off all the spiny needles down each side, there was plenty of moisture in it, he led his big gelding to it and staked him there, in no time the big palomino had licked and ate the thing clear to the ground, Wade scrounged around and found what little dried up grass he could and pulled it and brought to him as well, and patted him on the rump, "It ain't the best big fella, but you'll live to see another day" . . .

The night air had dropped a good forty degrees, sending a chill down his spine, pulling the bedroll up around his ears . . . There was a deathly quiet here in this valley, nothing seemed to move or make any sort of noise, there was no sign of life in it, only an occasional scorpion or two . . .

Wade rolled out early of the morning, there wasn't even a hint of daylight showing in the eastern horizon, he had picked out his route before dark the night before and marked it in his mind with the distant stars . . . The stars were bright, the big dipper well up into the sky, telling him it was late of the seasons . . . He saddled his horse and loaded his bedroll and saddle bags up and stepped into the saddle, the big gelding was refreshed from the cool nights rest and stepped out eagerly, Wade gave him his head and let him step out a good pace, he wanted to make as much ground as possible before the sun cooked them alive . . .

The sun was high above as they entered a different sort of ground, apparently there had been water here back in the spring months, as the ground went from powdery dry to a baked cracked land, cracks a good inch wide spread evenly throughout that left a puzzle looking landscape with thousands of one foot pieces, it was a hard packed ground, not even a cactus was evident . . . The heat waves danced across it, leaving a man blind to what lay ahead, the sun was bearing down with all it's might, the big gelding's head was no more than a foot off the ground, he was dragging his feet over in his strides, stumbling occasionally, Wade was walking beside him . . .

A cloud floated across the sky and momentarily blocked the rays of the sun, but the heat that lifted from under their feet was nauseous . . . He questioned his gamble on trying to cut through this barren wasteland, had he lost . . . Wade peered into the west, squinting his eyes against the blinding heat and waves that danced up from the floor of the valley, squinting harder he thought he could make out landscape not more than a mile away, they plodded on, the cloud quickly disappeared and Wade could see nothing ahead of them, an hour more of dragging across a no mans land as this, Wade could see a cedar and then another, and another higher off the ground, they had made it to the west rim, now they would have to find a place they could climb out . . . Working their way to the north, they came across an old washout, where the bank had given away during a spring rain probably, it had cut deep back into the wall of the rim, it was an old washout as the cedars had sprung up along it, making their way up it, steep as it was and rocky, a good thirty minutes later they topped out on the west rim . . .

A few clumps of Indian grass scattered about and Wade let the big gelding chew off a few bites . . . After a good hour of rest Wade stepped into the saddle, dark would be setting soon, and he wanted to make a path out into the open prairie looking for any sign of fresh tracks, tracks of Mary's horse, he had rode a good mile out into the prairie with no sign of tracks coming down from the north, he figured they would stay close to the rim as it led straight into Purgatory Wells . . . They found a small clump of cottonwoods that were growing around a small spring that held little water, it was a brackish water, but it was wet, he let his horse drink only little amounts at a time and pull him away and graze him on the green grass that was scattered about . . . Wade wet his bandana and washed his face and arms down, he felt like there was a pound of mud caked to him, he slowly filled his canteen, barely letting the lid drop below the waterline, only allowing the top fresher water run into it . . . He then turned it upside down, allowing the sediment to settle through the night, in the morning he would crack the lid and let what sediment had settled, run out and finish filling it the rest of the way with fresh water . . .

He had no clue as to the others camp, so he made no fire tonight . . . He felt he had cut them off by a day or two, maybe even more . . . Sleep came easy as he and the big gelding needed rest . . . Rising early the next morning Wade felt more at ease, there was no need to hurry, he would ride towards the north, he would ride cautiously, but he knew they were riding towards him now, he would pick the time and place now . . .

Wade pulled the Colt and Winchester both and cleaned them and checked each shell and all the working parts of each, he cleaned the sights of the Winchester and felt the smooth action of his Colt, putting it back in his holster and slipping the tie down back over the hammer . . . Stepping into the saddle they worked their way north, there was an old trail leading down from the north, no fresh tracks on it for weeks, they would be coming right down this trail he figured, he pulled reign and rode out to the west a good quarter of a mile, far enough off the trail not to be seen and close enough he could see anyone out in front of him, they rode on paralleling the trail . . .

Another day had passed as the evening sun went down . . . Wade found water and grass and made a quiet camp again with no fire . . . They had rode easy today and both were rested, Wade lay propped against a log on top of his bedroll, he could hear the palomino pulling grass and chewing it, he could hear a distant coyote testing his voice in the night air, the hoot of an owl, the rustling of grass in the evening breeze, a few leaves flickering as well, it was a peaceful sound, but Wade instantly set up, he just got a whiff of wood smoke drifting on the night air, he set quietly tuning his senses to the air, standing he could see no fire anywhere, but he was sure he had got wind of a fire, wood smoke floating in the evening breeze . . .

Leaving the big gelding tied in the grass and close to the water, he slid his Winchester from the scabbard and quietly disappeared into the darkness of the night . . . He followed the rim north, testing the occasional breeze often, after a mile he spotted a fire glowing, it was some distance a way still, and it was nestled in amongst some cedars, as the fire would disappear from time to time depending on what angle he worked towards it . . . There was sage and cedar scattered about the entire landscape here, broken rock outcroppings and cactus about, he worked his way within a good hundred yards of the fire, not knowing whose fire it might be . . . He could hear voices within the camp as he crawled on his belly the last portion, getting behind some rock and sagebrush hiding his whereabouts, he was no more than thirty feet away . . . He could peer under the brush and make out the camp, there was five bedrolls laid out, looking into the dark he could make out four men and Mary Franks, her hands tied over her head behind a small tree trunk . . . Anger grew within him like never before, he could feel his heart pounding in his chest and throat, he wanted to rush in there and start shooting and kill everyone of them, but that would risk a chance of Mary getting shot as well and maybe even himself, what good would he be to her if he got killed too . . .

Mary Franks was partially setting up, she couldn't set up because of her hands being tied behind her, her wrists were raw from the rawhide straps, her shoulders hurt from being over behind her head each night . . .

It was well into night, they had already ate and two of them were already in their bedrolls for the night, two of them were missing, Wade knew they were back on the trail waiting on him, these four had no reason to think otherwise . . .

Wade worked his way around to directly across from Mary, moving as a ghost in the night, not making a sound . . . Cupping his hands around his mouth he whistled into the night air, three times, the sound of a whippoorwill . . . Again he repeated it . . . Suddenly Mary looked straight towards him, something Wade had taught Mary, the sound of a whippoorwill was not uncommon, but a whippoorwill never stops with just three whistles, he will whistle nonstop for hours on end, and you never hear them other than the spring time . . .

Mary's heart took a leap within herself, it pounded hard in her chest, she knew it was Wade, she hade no doubts, she had hope, that he was still alive, and now she knew he was alive and he was here now . . . Her eyes watered up with tears . . .

Wade reached out and slowly moved a small branch that was hiding his face, his eyes met hers, he put his finger to his mouth and nodded to her and quickly disappeared into the darkness without a sound . . . Wade crawled back to a safer distance, but not more than fifty feet, he could still see into the camp . . .

He had laid in wait for a good hour without moving, it was near midnight when he saw one of the four men stand to his feet and stretch, and head into the woods, a good fifteen feet from where Wade lay, the man walked behind a tree and unbuckled his britches to relieve himself, Wade moved close, his eyes focused to the darkness of his hiding, picking up a limb the size and length of an axe handle, standing in the darkness of the shadows in line with which the trail he would walk back to camp, as he fastened his pants back up and headed towards the fire, he was caught off guard with a blow that smashed his nose into his forehead, landing with a thud flat on his back, out like a match in the wind . . .

Wade slipped around to the far side and worked his way up close to Mary . . . Mary had seen the other man walking into the woods and she knew he never came back, there was no way she could fall asleep tonight . . . Wade pulled his knife and cut the pigging strings from her wrists that had her tied to the tree, Mary didn't even know he was there until she felt her arms release from above her shoulders, she took a deep breath as it nearly scared her, Wade whispered softly to her, "It's ok, we'll be home soon" . . . as tears developed and ran down her cheeks, and he was gone again . . .

One of the other men stood up and headed out into the woods, but Wade was on the wrong side this time and wasn't going to be able to get there in time . . . He walked right into the other man lying on the ground, running back into camp hollering that Joe was out there knocked unconscious and his face was covered with blood, they all three had guns drawn, they were all standing in their sock feet, nervously staring out into the darkness in all directions, the big Mexican hollered for them to get Joe back in here to the camp, Wade leveled his Winchester and put a round into the middle of the coals of the fire, sending embers flying in all directions, in all the chaos that followed, Mary jumped to her feet and ran into the darkness, she had ran only about ten feet when she was hit hard from the side and landed face down with someone landing on top of her with a thud, nearly knocking the breath out of her, with an echoing booming of guns going off behind her, a hand over her mouth so she couldn't scream . . . It was the big Mexican, he scooped her up from the ground and carried her off into the brush and rocks, guns continued to echo into the darkness . . .

Wade had shot one man through the shoulder sending him to the ground and out of the fight, the only fight he had now was to stay alive, the other two fired into the darkness emptying their guns at shadows, Wade stepped up behind them while they were trying to reload, with his Winchester touching the back of one's head and his Colt on the neck of the other, a cocking sound that will send chills down any man's spine, "You boys can drop those guns and run as fast as you can, or I can shoot you in your tracks right here right now, it's your choice" . . .

"Don't shoot mister, we got no quarrel with you, we was just getting paid to do a job, you'll not see us again, please mister, don't kill us" . . .

"Start running now and don't even look back . . . GET!" . . . They took out through the sagebrush sock footed running as fast as they could muster . . .

Mary was gone as well as the big Mexican . . .

Wade stood motionless in the shadows, on the outskirts of their camp, his ears tuned to any sound of the night, since all the gunfire, there was not a sound to be heard for miles in any direction, he listened for a breath being taken, or the scraping of cloth on brush, but nothing, they were gone, they couldn't have gotten far, all the horses were still here . . . Wade stayed hid in the shadows, he couldn't give his location up at any cost, the big man was out there just waiting for Wade to step into the dim light of the fire . . . Daylight would soon overtake the darkness as Wade could see in the eastern horizon a reddish glow that marked the rising of the sun, he could then maybe pick up their tracks and follow them . . .

Mary could hardly breathe, his big hands were across her mouth and almost blocked her nose as well, he had a grip like a bear, he had drug her through the brush like a rag doll, her heart was beating like a drum, she could feel it in her chest and could hear it as well, she knew this man would kill her or worse, they were behind some rocks not far from the camp, she could vaguely see the remainder of the fire, she looked for Wade, but could see nothing, they knew not where any of them were, was Wade still alive, had they shot him, maybe he lay back there needing her help, bleeding to death . . .

Daylight over took the dawn and Wade was crawling on his knees amongst the sage brush looking for sign of which way they went, keeping out of sight, for he knew the Mexican would be looking for an easy shot from somewhere, Wade couldn't risk any chances, he found their trail, it was easy to read as Mary had been drug nearly all the way, her feet kicking in the dirt as they went, peering up through the short broken clumps of sage brush he could see that they had entered a clump of broken rocks protruding up from the desert floor . . . Wade crawling on his belly took a wide loop out around, working his way towards the rocks from a different angle so he would come in from the opposite side, he knew the Mexican would be watching for him, although they didn't know who was alive or dead after all the shooting took place . . .

Wade took a good two hours working his way around and came in from behind, he scoured the ground as best he could and found no tracks leaving, so he figured they were holed up in the rocks, still on his belly he studied the entire surroundings, he worked his way to the edge of the rocks and stood up, he could still see no sign of tracks, they had to be around the front side, with his Colt in hand he slipped around the face of the granite rock, peering around the edge he saw them, the big Mexican's back was turned to him, Mary was in front of him, using her as a shield . . .

Wade stepped out, Colt leveled off at the man: "Let her go and maybe you will live" . . .

The big man whirled around in a split second, he was holding a knife to Mary's throat, it was a fighting man's knife, a smooth handle made of bone with a large bolster to protect a man's hand in fights, a blade of Damascus steel, Wade could see the swirl marks in the metal of it, it was sharpened and tapered to a needle like point, and was sharp on both sides . . .

Blood started to trickle down Mary's neck as the point of the knife protruded into her skin with the slightest pressure: "I think you better drop your gun Señor or I end her life with the slightest movement of my arm" . . .

Wade's colt was aimed directly at the mans head, but he knew that even if he made a clean shot, he could sever her throat falling to the ground . . .

The man was big, a good seventy five pounds on Wade, his forearms were wrapped with leather gauntlets laced together on the underside, Wade could see knife marks on the man's biceps, it was obvious the fellow had been in more than one knife fight in his life, and Wade could tell he was proud of it . . .

"Señor, you drop your gun belt now or I do her" . . . as he pressured the knife ever lightly more and Mary's blood started to trickle down the edge of the blade running to his fingers, and he smiles at Wade . . .

Wade puts the Colt back in the holster and unbuckles the belt and just as he tosses it to the ground, he palmed the handle of his own knife and slid it out, Wade standing there waving his own knife in an invitation . . .

The big Mexican scoffs and laughs at Wade, but Wade knew this man would want it like this, he knew the big man had all the confidence in the world that he could and would take Wade with little ease . . . The big man tosses Mary to the side like she weighed nothing, Mary landed on the rocks hitting her head causing a nasty cut just above her eye, she laid limp and motionless on the rocks, Wades anger grew within him, but he knew he had to stay calm, he could not fight this man in a fit of anger, this would be a fight for his life, his life and that of Mary . . .

The Mexican whipped his knife in the air as a swordsman would do and then tossed the knife to the other hand and done the same procedure, an act that would instill fear in most of his opponents that he could use a knife in either hand effectively, intimidation that did not affect Wade, for he was not a novice with a knife himself, a trade he had learned from his Apache friend . . .

Wade just took a good grip on his knife and motioned with his left hand to come on, there was nothing fancy of Wades approach, but he could handle a knife as well . . .

The Mexican would not make one fatal cut, he would feint in and out making quick moves flicking his knife making small wounds that would bleed profusely, he would be like a cat playing with a mouse, this was a game for him, he enjoyed making his prey suffer . . . Wade knew he would have to outsmart him, for he knew he could never over power the man . . .

Wade looked towards Mary lying on the heap of rocks, motionless . . .

"Señor, I will enjoy your woman when I am finished with you, she would not want you after she has had me anyway amigo" as he laughs . . .

"You better worry about getting past me first, I believe you have bit off more than you can chew" as Wade made a lunge forward with his knife . . .

The big man blocking the stab easily and taking a flick at Wade with his own, but Wade had dodged his cut as well, the big man feinted in with his right and Wade quickly stepped to the left, but the Mexican quickly tossed his knife and caught it with his other hand making a swiping cut that caught the back of Wades right arm, leaving a two inch cut, not deep, just a slash through the skin, it was hot and the mingle of blood and sweat made it look much worse than it was, the sweat running into the wound made it sting . . . The big man came again catching Wade across the right shoulder and again nipping his right side . . . The Mexican smiled: "I will bleed you like a pig Señor" . . .

Wade could feel the blood trickle down his side . . . The big man's confidence was high and he knew he could end it anytime, Wade knew it was time to turn the tables, he faked a lunge at the big man, he blocked it and made a hard stab of his own at Wades chest, Wade stepped to his right and used the mans own weight to rush past him, and tossed his own knife to his other hand and made a wide swing, catching him just above his right elbow, Wade could feel his knife hitting bone with a swing as hard as he could muster, hitting him not more than an inch above his elbow, severing the tendons, the big Mexican quickly turned to face Wade, anger building in his eyes, but his knife drops to the ground, he reaches down to pick it back up, but his fingers and hand can't clasp it, he had lost reactions of his right forearm, it dangled like a string, blood dripping from his fingers, the Mexican quickly picks up his knife with his left hand, Wade caught the big man looking down at his feet and smiling, Wade had felt a rock behind him as he turned, slightly leaning back he could tell the rock was just above his knees, the big man charged knowing that Wade would fall backwards over the rock, Wade scrambled backwards and fell to his back, but rolling on over and coming back to his feet in an instant, the big man was shocked to see Wade roll back to his feet so quickly, but he couldn't stop his charge, his knife was held low thinking his opponent would be laying on the ground, Wade quickly shoved him past his position and taking the butt end of the big knife, swung with all his power, smashing the butt of his knife into the base of his skull making a popping sound like hitting a block of wood, the big Mexican landing face down into a pile of rocks, he struggled to get up but collapsed back onto his chest . . . Wade walked over and picks up the Mexican's knife and tosses it over the side of the rim into the canyon floor below . . . Wade was standing over the big man, his heart pounding, his breathing hard from the fight, he could feel the blood trickle down his arm and side, every ounce of his being wanted to kill this man, he wanted vengeance, adrenaline was coursing through his veins, but suddenly his thoughts changed to that of Mary, and now killing this man seemed immaterial . . .

Wade ran to Mary who was just now regaining consciousness, he had his bandana out and sopping the blood from her forehead, she was dizzy and her head ached, her eyes were watery . . . Wade held her in his arms, her eyes quickly regained focus as she yells: "Wade"!!

Wades back was to the big man, but he had heard the cocking of a revolver, instinctively turning on his heels, he could see the Mexican pulling a hidden revolver from the inside of his boot, fumbling with his left hand, but before he got it leveled off, Wade still holding his knife, flung it at the Mexican with all his might, the knife hitting it's target, catching him two inches into the bottom of his sternum and the weight of the big knife drove clear to the hilt leaving nothing but the handle sticking out, the big Mexican gasping for his final breaths, still trying to gain control of the short revolver but loosing his grip on it as he drops it to the ground, then he drops to his knees and finally collapses face down in the sandy desert . . .

Wade turns back to Mary who nearly collapses in his arms, crying uncontrollably . . . Her arms around his neck with a grip that would choke a bear . . .

"Its ok now Mary, it's ok, we're safe and we'll be heading back home shortly" . . .

"Wade, there's two more of them back on the trail waiting for you" . . .

"They won't be a problem for us now, they won't be expecting us from this direction, do you know where they are holed up waiting for me?"

"Yes, but what if they see us coming?"

"Then they will know the rest of their gang is dead or gone and will probably run themselves" . . .

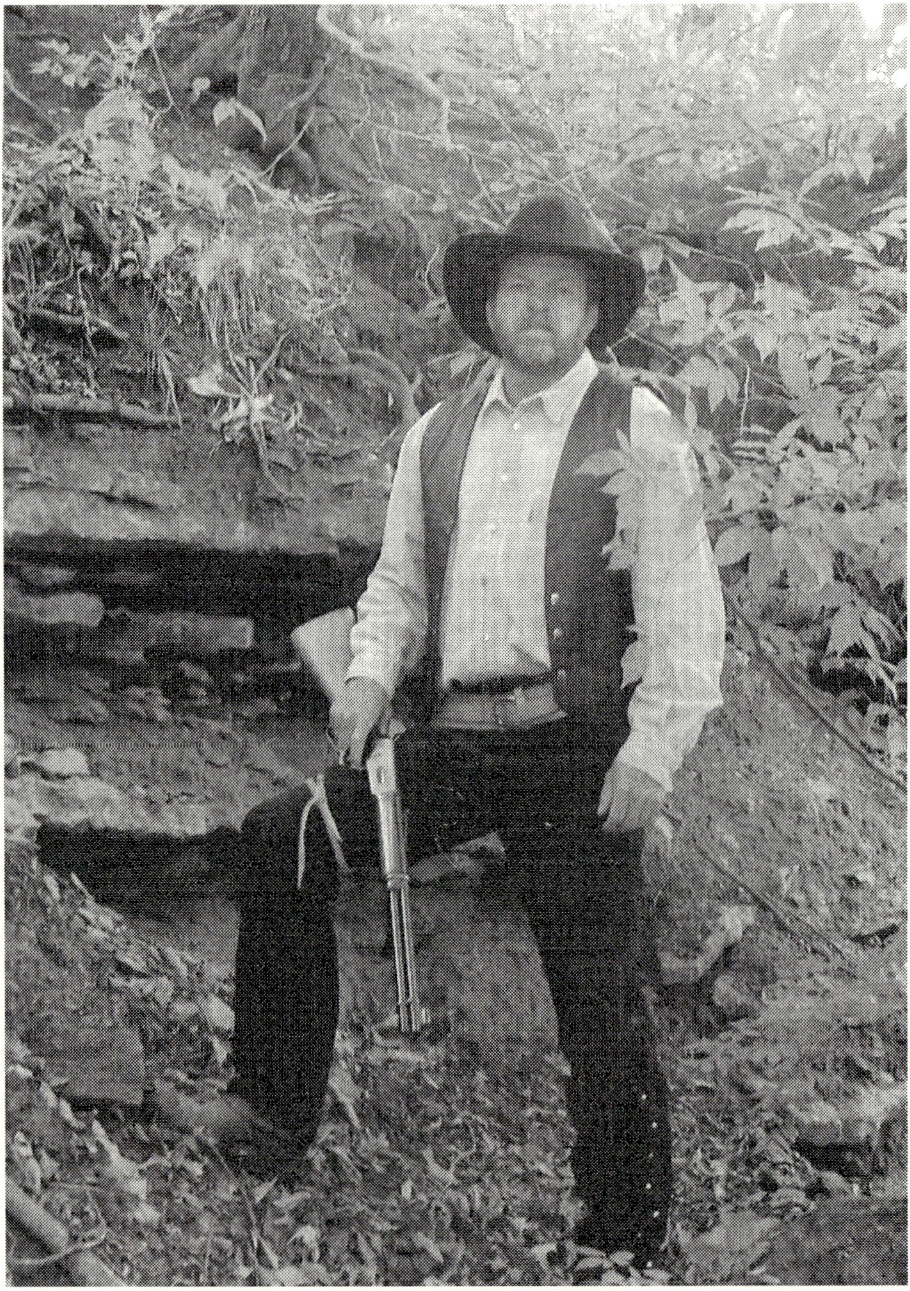

Chapter 15

Wade and Mary returned to camp and retrieved Mary's bedroll and things, then turned the other men's horses loose into the prairie, and scrounged up what supplies and grub were left then walked back to Wades camp and saddled his palomino and headed north . . . Their two horses seemed to be glad to see each other and stepped out at a good pace heading home . . . They only had a few hours of daylight left, but they both wanted to be shy of this area, Wade had rode several miles out of the way and found a rocky oasis that was obscure from the main trail and built a fire and had fresh hot coffee and jerky for their supper, night fall had settled in and the fire felt great, but more than that, was the companion they each shared, dark overtook the dusk of the evening as they pulled their bedrolls together and crawled in for the night, it was the best rest they both had had for weeks . . . It had been nearly two months since they had slept together . . .

Morning had rolled in with the promise of a beautiful day, the sun had already crested the eastern horizon, the sky was a vivid blue and not even a scant of a cloud, Wade smiling at himself as he still lay in his bedroll and the sun was up . . . Mary was still asleep, her breathing relaxed and peaceful, but Wade felt he couldn't let her sleep any longer, he reached over and traced the outline of her face with his finger, her eyes cracked open slightly, but Wade could see the smile in them, as they had a gleam that he loved to see . . .

"Good morning Mary Franks" . . .

Her eyes are fully open and a bright gleam in them which matches the smile on her face, she slides her arm under his head and pulls herself over to him, His arm goes around behind her back and pulls her close and holds her tight . . .

"I am not ready to get up Mr. Tavner, I haven't slept that good since you left with the herd, I just want to lay here a bit longer" . . .

Wade continues to hold her tight, the birds are singing in the morning breeze, the warmth of the sun sifts into their camp, the rustle of a desert cottontail stirs in the sagebrush, the screech of a hawk in flight high above the desert floor looking for his morning meal . . .

They break camp with a chore ahead of them, knowing that two more men are back on the trail in ambush waiting for them . . .

"Wade, it's probably a days ride to where they left us to wait for you, it was a narrow passage through some rocky areas of buttes, they were to climb up in the rocks and wait there" . . .

"I think I know the place Mary, and we will come in from the north of it and make a surprise visit ourselves" . . .

Riding throughout the day, talking as they hadn't seen each other for some time, and it seemed like it had been a very long time to them both . . . Wade had told her how well the cattle had sold and all the mischief of four young men, and how he had grown fond of each of them as they were good boys, who would make fine men in due time . . .

Mary talked of the Mexican shooting Ramos in the back and shooting Roscoe . . . Mary's eyes had filled with tears, "It was as though he enjoyed shooting them Wade, it was awful, I've never seen a man like that before" . . . She was thrilled that Roscoe was still alive when Wade got there, she figured that he had died after they took her . . .

The sun was well behind their backs as the day had disappeared before them . . . Wade had taken them well out of the way from the normal trail that followed the rim of the canyon, the sun would be down in a couple of hours . . . Wade normally would make camp well before dark, but he had a destination to make, he could see the rise in the land that lay ahead of them, he knew that was where their ambush awaited them . . .

"Wade, can't we just ride around them and let them stay and wait for no one"?

"This has to be finished, we don't want to ride all the way back home looking over our shoulders wondering if they are behind us" . . .

They made camp a good quarter mile from the rocky pass, it would be a dark camp, with no fire tonight, they chewed on some jerky and a sourdough hunk of stale bread, they wouldn't risk a fire being seen . . .

The night settled in with darkness, it was a dry moon overhead, only a crescent, putting off little light, stars were bright in the desert sky . . . Wade stood at the edge of camp peering into the darkness towards the rocky cliffs just ahead of them, he spotted what he was looking for, a dim glow of a campfire, he knew they were there . . . He walked back to camp and set down beside Mary, there were a couple of rocks scattered about that made decent settings, Wade had smoothed out an area and had laid out the bedrolls, Mary was about to turn in for the night, when Wade picked up his Winchester . . .

"I'll be back shortly, they have a fire going and I plan to pay them a visit tonight" . . .

"Wade Tavner, if you think for one minute that I am going to set here and wonder all night long, if you will be returning or not, then you have been smoking some of that loco weed for sure, if you are going over there, then I am too"!!

"Mary, I"

"SHHHHHHHSH, not another word of it Wade" as she sets back up and pulls on her boots . . . "Give me the rifle, you got your colt, don't forget you taught me how to shoot" . . .

"And do you plan on shooting a man if you have too" . . .

"If I have too"!!!

Wade knew there was no need in arguing further, he thought to himself, he should have waited until she was asleep and slipped out into the night . . .

They worked their way around through the sage brush, working up from the north side of the rocky cliff, they would more than likely be asleep by now, or at least setting back relaxed, leaning against a backrest, looking into the fire, blinding themselves from the dark shadows of a night . . .

They were within twenty feet of the camp, on their hands and knees, making not a sound, an owl hooted from across their camp, not even the night watch of mother nature had noticed their appearance . . .

Wade raised up so he could see into the camp, both men were stretched out fast asleep, standing to his feet he motioned for Mary to come along with him, tiptoeing right into their camp, Wade reached down and took both their side arms from beside their bedrolls, a horse nickered close by, but neither men moved from their slumber, Wade stuck both of their revolvers in his belt, Mary was standing there with the Winchester pointed directly at them, Wade took his Colt and placed it on the back of one of the sleeping men's head, directly behind his ear and motioned for Mary to do the same to the other man, the cocking sound of a gun placed directly behind your ear is quite an awakening, the one man instinctively slid his hand for his pistol, but it wasn't there . . .

Wade smiled, "You boys looking for me"?

"Uh, uh, well" . . .

The one man tried to speak but words seemed to be lodged in his throat . . .

The other man said: "Shut up Deek" . . . and he looked at Wade in disbelief and anger . . . "Carlos will kill you and" then he realized Mary was holding the other gun on them . . .

"Gents, Carlos ain't going to rescue you here and he's never going to hurt anyone again, and it's just the two of you left now, so it seems that you have very few options at this point, one being, you can get real stupid and I'll have to kill you both, or you can get on your horses right now and ride out, and you better be riding in a direction that does not allow me to ever cross trails with you again, because if I ever meet you fellows again, Mary here may not be along and there will be blood shed, the guns stay with me" . . .

Deek jumps up and grabs his boots and pulls them on, "Mister, you don't need to worry about me no more, let me get my horse and I will be on my way sir" . . .

Wade looks at the other, "Your choice, you going with your buddy here, or you want to take your chance with me"?

"I'm going, heck, this ain't my fight anyway" . . . As he pulls the covers back, but quickly pulled a knife from under the bedroll . . .

Wade saw the flash of metal in the dim light of the fire and the moon, and quickly smashed his knuckles straight into the man's face, Wade could feel the crushing of his nose under the pressure of the blow, the man tried to regain his efforts, but before Wade could even get to his feet, Mary had stepped in and shoved the barrel of the Winchester straight into his face, leaving a ring shaped impression on the man's forehead, her finger on the trigger, the hammer was cocked, she was shaking mad, her teeth were clinched tight, her heart was throbbing in her chest and throat, "I'll kill you if you as much as blink, I swear I will" . . .

Wade had a look of as much surprise as the man lying on the ground . . .

"Are you so sure you want to die tonight? I truly don't think she is bluffing here mister" . . .

Blood pouring down across the man's face, his hand pressed against his nose, blood dripping between his fingers, but he manages to get to his feet and find his way to his horse . . .

Mary held the Winchester on him until he was fully mounted and on his way . . .

Wade listened well into the night, for he could hear the pounding of the horses hooves well after they had left . . .

Mary set down on a rock with a huge sigh of relief, and finally laid down the rifle . . .

"I am so glad that is all over with" . . .

"Me too" . . . But Wade still had a knot in his stomach that he did not share with Mary . . .

Walking back to their own camp, things felt much more relaxed, sleep would not come easy for either of them as all the excitement had them well awake . . .

It was still dark of the night, a couple of hours before daylight would creep into the existence of the day, Wade reached over and woke Mary, her eyes opened with a look of concern of why he would wake her while it was still so dark . . .

"I can't sleep, there is something we need to do as soon as we can" . . .

"What is it Wade"? With even more of a concerned look . . .

"Mary, I have thought of this before, but I had never said anything about it, and you have never mentioned it to me, but surely you have thought of it as well . . . But after all that has happened lately, and the thoughts that I might have lost you" . . .

"Wade, just say what you want" . . .

"Mary Frances Franks, I wish for you to be my wife, I wish for us to get married as soon as we can" . . .

A gleam lightens in Mary's eyes but are quickly flooded with tears, tears of joy . . .

But Wade, being a man, doesn't know the meaning of the tears and has a concerned look upon his face . . .

Mary setting up from their bedroll, and drying her eyes, "Mr. Tavner, what on earth would make you think I would want to marry a man who attracts as much trouble as you"?

Wade with an astonished look on his face, a look of puzzlement and of unassuredness, "I just thought uh I uh, well I" . . .

Mary reaches over and puts her hand on his mouth and keeps him from stumbling more with a lack of speech, and laughs . . .

"Wade Tavner, I would give my life to be your wife for the rest of our days" as she nearly jumps into his arms and they both fall back into their bedrolls, lips pressed together with passion as never before . . .

Morning rolled in with a sunrise to match the feeling of their hearts with as much warmth as well . . . A quick breakfast and they were saddled and on their way . . .

The horses were stepping out at a good pace as well . . .

"Mary, there is a town a good day's ride due north of here, we could make it by nightfall and I believe they have a judge in town and more than likely a circuit preacher some where abouts, I want to do this" . . .

"You're leading the way, I'm going wherever you are, are you sure you don't want to wait until we get back to Silver Creek Springs"?

"Nope, nothing in Silver Creek Springs to wait on, I want you to be my wife as soon as possible" . . .

Wade seemed to push the horses at a good pace throughout the day, stopping at noon for a quick lunch and letting the horses rest briefly, they were good horses with strong stamina, horses that were used to a good days work and could cover a lot of ground . . .

Riding into Miles Gulch a good hour before dark fell, reigning into the livery stable and stalling their horses for the night, paying the hostler two bits for good hay and a couple scoops of oats, brushing down their mounts and cleaning the dust and dirt from them, finishing with setting the saddles on a log rail and laying their saddle blankets upside down on top of the saddles to dry, so they would be fresh for saddling . . .

Wade and Mary walked down the main street and stepped into the hotel and procured a room for the night and went up and cleaned up a bit . . . They came back down and asked the hotel clerk of the best place to eat in town and if there was a Reverend or Judge in town . . .

"Why yes sir, we got both, in fact both are in town tonight, you might find the circuit preacher over at Lou's, and that's the best place to eat anyway, there ain't nothing fancy about it, but clean as a pin and good food, and well, Mr. Hawkins, the judge, you might check Kate's saloon, he sort of likes to hang out down there and play a few hands of cards of the evening hours" . . .

Mary stepped up, "And what would this Reverend be called"?

"He goes by Pastor Bill, Bill Larkin would be his full name ma'am" . . .

They headed on down the boardwalk as the boards creaked under each step, meeting a few folks as they strode along, friendly folks, folks who would tip a hat and have an evening greeting for those they passed along the way, it made them both smile as it was a friendly town . . .

Stepping into Lou's Eating Establishment, it was a clean place, tables set nicely around in an organized fashion, white linens set on the tables, freshly clean and ironed, with napkins set at each chair, chairs pushed up under the tables, nothing out of place . . .

A healthy looking woman of a good fifty years of age stepped up and asked to seat them, the place was nearly full, only a few tables left, but Wade had already picked out a table towards the back of the room, facing the front, and he asked her if that one would suffice, and she escorted them to the table and took their order for cold sweetened tea . . .

She brought the tea back out and introduced herself as Lou, Wade quickly looked up and she smiled back at him, "It's Lou, short for Louise, and I prefer Lou, is that ok with you"?

Wade smiled back: "You can go by anything you want ma'am, would it matter if I didn't like it"?

"I don't like ma'am either, it's Lou" . . .

"Well Lou, before we order, could you tell us if Pastor Bill would be in the place"?

"Well sir, he's not here right this minute, but he should be along anytime, and when he does, that table right here beside you is where he'll be setting, he sort of likes to set back here and watch folks come and go and see out on the street as well, he's a short fella with not much hair on top" . . .

Wade and Mary both ordered the special of roast beef with tators and gravy which was served with hot rolls and fresh churned butter . . .

By the time they had finished, Pastor Bill had came in and took his usual table beside them . . .

After getting acquainted, they made arrangements to meet him at eight o'clock sharp the next morning and get themselves hitched . . .

They strolled back to the Hotel and paid five cents for a hot bath each, the bath felt good to them both as they had been living out on the prairie for some time, with the dust settling in every spot on a persons body . . . Mary had washed her hair and was towel drying it as Wade stepped back into the room, he was clean and had a fresh shirt on, his leather vest fit neatly around his chest, Mary's eyes had a pure gleam of delight in them . . . Wade looked at Mary with her hair wet and hanging down past her shoulders, combed out neatly, she smelled of sweet perfume of lilacs . . . He walked over and put his arm around behind her back and pulled her close, she felt even better than she smelt, his other hand slid behind her head and his fingers mingled within her soft clean hair as he pulled her face close to his . . .

The soft down mattress felt warm and cozy to their bones, from sleeping on the ground over the past weeks, the sheets were pure white and clean, the sounds of the street out front quickly faded as they both fell fast asleep . . .

Morning rolled in with sunshine filtering into the room through the window that overlooked the main street of town . . . Mary set up in bed, hardly believing she had slept past the sunrise, rubbing her eyes open, thinking she hadn't slept that good in a long time, But suddenly realizing, Wade was gone, she quickly looked around the room and his boots and holster were gone, he had gotten up earlier and was already out . . .

Wade had left as soon as the sun was peering over the distant horizon, he had things to do, and he wished to let Mary sleep as long as she wished . . . He had not a ring for her hand, and wanted one in the worst way . . . The storeowners would be out opening shops and sweeping the boardwalks early, but Wade could find not one ring in the town for his bride to be . . . He made his way to the end of the boardwalk and walked on past the livery to the local blacksmith . . . A burly looking man, thick arms with dark hair, hair that looked oily shiny and laid back over the man's scalp, a chest as broad as an axe handle . . .

"The name's Wade Tavner sir" . . .

"Benjamin Barker, and what can I do for you sir" as he extends his hand . . .

Wade extends his as well for a friendly handshake, grasping the big man's hand was like gripping a hold on a grizzly . . .

"Benjamin, I need to make something" . . .

"You a blacksmith er ya? I'm not rightly fond of loaning my tools out to strangers" . . .

"I understand that sir, but I'd be doing a small task right here under your watchful eye" . . .

"And what is it that you'd be a making" . . .

"Well Benjamin, I'd like to forge a ring" . . .

"Well how big a ring ya talking, one for pulling logging chains or wheelwright ring or what you got in mind"?

Wade laughs: "Well sir, a ring just big enough to fit over my little finger" . . .

The big man gives a short laugh that shakes his belly, with a look of concern of whether this fellow is pulling his leg or what . . .

"Let me explain here, I am getting married this morning, and I don't have a wedding ring for my woman, and their ain't a ring in this town to be had, so I'd like to at least make one of metal" . . .

The blacksmith laughs: "Well we can fix you right up here shortly" . . .

He brings out a short strap of quarter inch iron, looks at Wade's little finger and fetches a half inch round rod a foot long and clamps it tight in the vise, then hands Wade a small dinger's hammer and a set of long handled pincers . . . "You set that quarter strap in that forge there until she's good and hot mind ya, don't take her out till she's red, then take them there pincers and set that strap atop that rod and you just shape it right around it, overlap the ends a good half inch or so and lop it off, slide it back off that rod and re-heat her until she's red again, put it back on that rod with the overlap on the top and you mesh them together with that there dinger I give ya, you'll end up with an endless loop of steel" . . .

Wade done as instructed and finished it with light ding marks all around it in a hammered look, then they heated it back up until it was red again and then dropped it into a bucket of oil . . .

"That will put the temper in it and will last forever, and when you take it out of that oil, you can buff it into a real shine with that oil burned into it like that and will leave it with a bluish hue to it" . . .

Wade was right proud of his gift for Mary . . .

When Wade returned to the Hotel, Mary was standing on the boardwalk looking up and down the main street in both directions . . . Wade slipped up behind her: "You looking for something"?

"You" . . .

Wade simply smiled, pulling his watch from his vest pocket, "I believe we got time for some breakfast Ms. Franks" . . .

"You not going to tell me what you've been up to this fine morning Mr. Tavner"

"Not a chance of it" . . . as he lifts out his arm to escort her to Lou's place, Mary slides her arm inside his as he gently squeezes down on hers, which gave her a great feeling of security . . .

Breakfast was good, and now time to meet the reverend . . .

Wade and Mary reached the steps to the church and Wade paused: "Last chance for you to change your mind Ms. Franks" . . .

"You wouldn't be so lucky" as she smiled back at him . . .

The preacher just stepped to open the door and they greeted him: "Good morning pastor Bill" . . .

"Please call me Bill, just Bill, I have an idea you might both like, out back of our little church here, setting on the bank of West Creek, we have a small gazebo, and well it's such a beautiful morning with the sunshine and nice weather, well I thought you might rather have your vows performed out there" . . .

Mary looked at Wade, "I would love that, what do you think"?

"Outdoors is fine with me Mary, I thought you might want a church building wedding" . . .

"I believe outdoors under the sun and blue skies fits us better, I can't think of a better way to become your wife Mr. Tavner" . . .

So it was done, after the vows were said, Wade pulled his hand made ring from his pocket and placed it on Mary's finger, it couldn't have fit better, it was a thing of beauty on her finger . . .

Mary's eyes filled with tears as she pulled him close and kissed him and held him tight with her arms around his neck and his behind her back . . . There was a feeling of warmth that ran deep in both of their bodies, it seemed to run from the pit of their stomachs, up through the middle of their hearts and deep into each others souls . . .

Shortly after their vows were said and a short visit with Pastor Bill and his wife, they were saddled and heading home . . .

Mary toiled with the ring on her finger, as she would spin it around her finger with her thumb, it felt great . . .

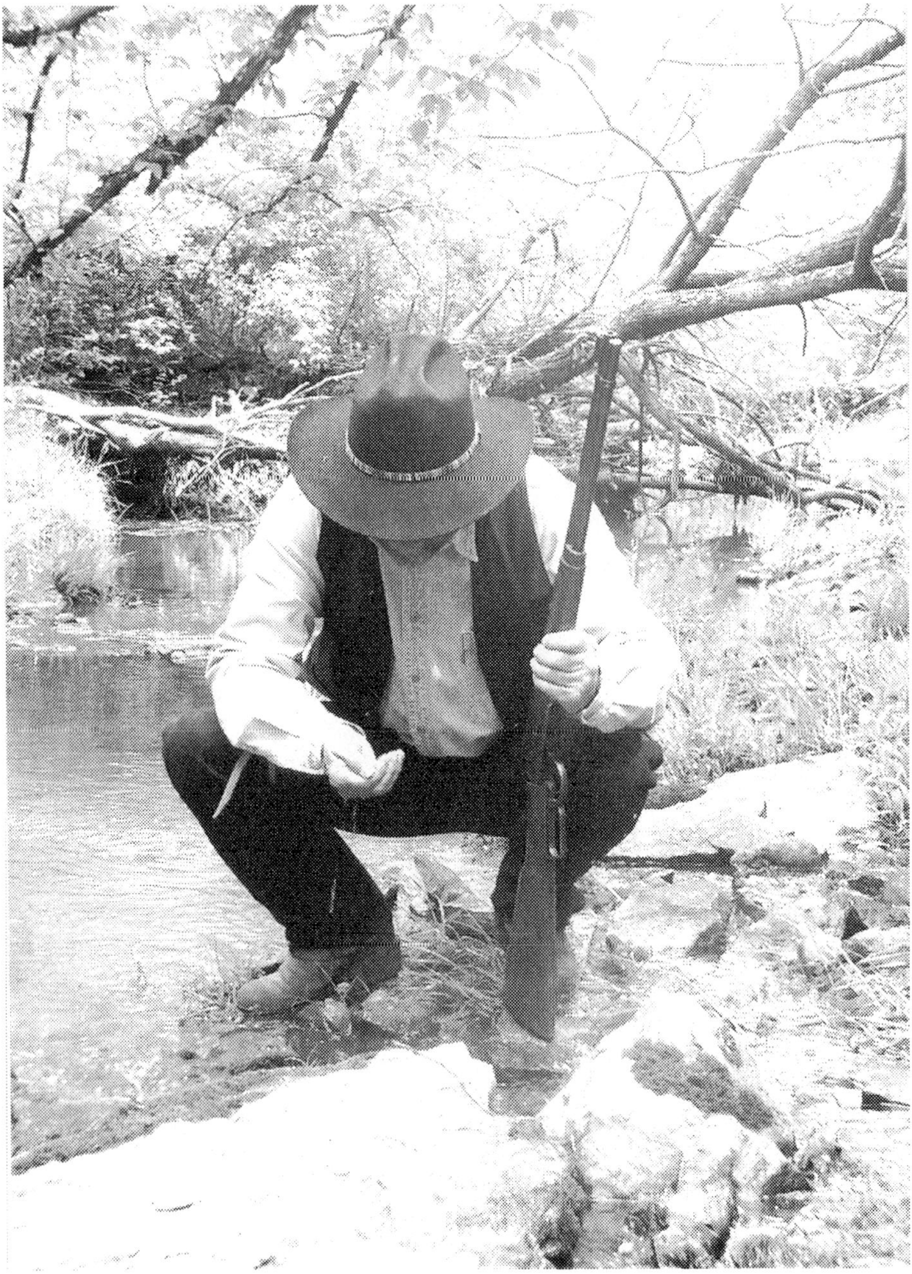

Chapter 16

It seemed they had only been riding for a few hours before the dawn was settling in, they had covered good ground for the short few hours they had rode today . . . Camp was set along side a small stream, water was fresh and cold, there was plenty of wood for a fire, the landscape had changed greatly during the last couple of days, they had gotten out of the prairie land and were now in some of the foot hills areas, pine trees were scattered about, the scents had changed from that of dust and sage to a fresher pine smell that drifted in the air, the stream they set camp beside reminded them of home, it churned and gurgled against the rocks as it meandered by, a relaxing sound . . . They had bought fresh supplies in Miles Gulch, so supper was good with sliced slab bacon mingled in with a pot of beans and fresh coffee boiled on the open fire . . .

"Say it again Wade"?

"Say what again"?

She smiles at him: "Mary Frances Tavner, don't that have a grand sound to it, or Mrs. Wade Tavner" . . .

Wade smiles back as he tosses another stick of dead pine on the fire, the coals were red hot and just right for cooking, the smell of wood smoke mingled with the smell of the bacon searing made them both hungry, two tin plates were setting on a rock beside the fire, Wade dishes up a helping for them both as they settle down leaned up against a log . . . Dark over took the camp, nothing but the glow of the fire, the sounds of the day changed to the sounds of the night, a distant owl hooted to his mate, crickets along the creek answered to each others calls, a lone coyote echoed into the darkness, only the stream remained constant of sound . . . Wade stoked the fire with larger chunks of wood for the night, and crawled into the bedrolls and huddled in for the night . . . The fire crackled and embers of sparks drifted effortlessly upwards towards the sky above . . .

They had covered a lot of country and were getting into the higher ranges, it had been a quiet day of riding, too quiet, Mary dug her heels into the ribs of her black and jumped in front of Wade, then pulled reign over in front of him, and blocked his way . . .

"Wade, you going to tell me what's eating at you"?

Wade gives her a forced smile, "Nothing, I'm just thinking about getting home and getting the cows all rounded back up" as he starts to move past her . . .

Mary reigns around again, "I don't buy that Mr. Tavner, I know something is gnawing at you, you might as well spill here and now" . . .

Wade lifts the reigns and steps down from the saddle and helps Mary from hers . . .

"I didn't want to worry you with this, but Mary, four men tried to kill me, four more were to get rid of you in a way worse than killing, that wasn't no coincidence you know" . . .

"But Wade, those men are either dead or running still" . . .

"Mary, those men weren't acting on their own, they were doing a job they had been paid to do, and whoever paid them is still out there . . . I think I know why they wanted us out of the way, but I don't rightly know who" . . .

"Why Wade, why did someone want us gone, we have bothered no one" . . .

"Mary, when I settled in Three Valleys Ranch, the first week I was there, I found gold buried in the stream behind our cabin, I have told no one, and will take it to my grave that way, but a couple of days before I left to drive the cattle for sale, up in the high country I found some diggings, some one had been up there test mining, there were two men, one man had stayed a couple of nights up there, the other man just seemed to be overseeing what was found . . . I noticed his tracks, and still have them in my mind, when I got home and you were gone, I searched the entire area again, I found those same tracks watching from above when they took you . . . His tracks led back to town" . . .

Mary with a concerned look, "Do you know who it was"?

"No, his tracks were wiped out in the traffic in town, but whoever it was, I am sure is still there, and he wants us dead, and the closer we get to home, the more dangerous it will be, Mary, I can't get you hurt, if it hadn't been for me, you would still be living with your Aunt and Uncle in a warm cozy safe home back in Ft. Douglas, out of harms way" . . .

Mary's eyes looked as if they could throw daggers, Wade had never seen her look mean before, her voice gets a tad bit louder as she jabs her finger in Wade's chest "Wade Tavner, let's get one thing straight right now, I wish to be no where but with you, now or before or anytime afterwards, I have no intentions of running at the first sign of trouble, now if you think for one minute that I want to go back to Ft. Douglas where it might be safe, then you don't know squat"!!

Wade grabs her finger on about the tenth stab in his chest . . . "Let's go home Mrs. Tavner" as he smiles at her and hands her the reigns to the black, rubbing his chest with his hand, "That hurts you know" . . .

She smiles back at him: "You haven't seen nothing yet, just go down that road again and see" . . .

The conversation of the rest of the day was of a pleasant tone, but Wade had kept a close eye out for anything out of the normal, and he rode off the normal route that would be taken by most travelers, he changed directions often, riding in a zig zag fashion, and kept a close eye on the ground for fresh tracks . . .

Camp was set in a thick grove of pines, Wade built only a small fire of dead limbs, tender that put off little smoke . . . Mary knew his ways and kept quiet, she knew everything he done was for their safety, she had learned a great deal by just observing the way Wade went about things . . . Mary slept soundly, but she knew Wade would hear every sound of the night . . .

Mary awoke and Wade was gone from the bedroll, fire ready with a small blaze and cups of coffee warming close to the flames, his bedroll beside her as though he hadn't even laid down in it . . . Wade had climbed to a higher point and was looking out over the horizon, watching for any sign of movement, checking the wind for any hint of wood smoke, but the light breeze was against him for that . . .

Wade walked back into camp as Mary handed him the freshly boiled coffee and a tin of sliced bacon, fried crisp, "You see anything"?

"Nope, it all seems quiet, I think we will be home either late tonight or early tomorrow, and I don't know about you, but I am more than ready to be home" . . .

"We will have a ton of work to do getting all the livestock rounded back up as they knocked down the corrals at the end of the valley" . . .

It was getting close to noon, Wade had been thinking of stopping for a quick lunch and resting the horses a bit, he had been looking for the right place to pull up, when suddenly he saw a glimpse of light flash up on the cliff in the thick trees just ahead of them, he instantly dug his right spur into the ribs of the big palomino slamming him into the front shoulder of Mary's black nearly knocking her horse off his feet, Mary hit the ground with a thud, Wade clearing his horse at the same time grabbing Mary around the waist as she tried to regain her feet under her and diving behind some rocks and trees, landing on her back nearly knocking the wind from her, the echoing boom of a rifle shattered the silence of the mountains, a bullet ripped into the ground where Wade was just a second before, a second shot rang out glancing off the rocks they just dove behind, sending debris just passed Mary's head, Wade cursed . . .

Wade lifted slightly to look above them, another shot boomed into the afternoon sunshine, hitting close to it's target, Wade was bitter mad, here they set, pinned down, his Winchester still on his horse and no way to get it as the horses had run off a good hundred yards from the excitement, whoever was shooting at them was a good hundred yards up the steep slope, looking down on them, his colt would do him no good at that distance . . .

Peering between two of the rocks he made out the man's position, he could see him move slightly . . . Wade removes his colt, and unbuckles his belt, and hands it to Mary . . .

"You see that short pine up there right next to that big bald faced rock, when I say now, you empty that colt into that tree, keep your head down, shoot between these two rocks, keep pulling that trigger until you run out, then reload it, keep your head down Mary" . . .

"And just what are you planning on doing" . . .

"Mary, I'm going for my horse and the rifle" . . .

"Wade" . . .

Wade shook his head . . .

"We can't set here and wait on him, get ready, now" . . .

Mary set up and opened fire with the colt as fast as she could thumb the hammer back, Wade jumped to his feet and took off at a run as fast as his feet would carry him, guns booming behind him as he ran, he reached the big horse at a run, the horse spooked only slightly but Wade hit the saddle with a leap and dug his spurs in and disappeared into the thickness of the trees, Mary's black was close behind . . .

The man on the lookout perch felt lost now, he had missed his target and now they were split apart and both had guns, he knew not where Wade had gone or where he would be. But he did know Wade Tavner would be coming after him, so he gave up his ambush attempt and scrambled back up the cliff and got on his horse and headed out as fast as he could ride . . .

Wade tied the horses off, close to some water and green grass under foot, and worked his way around the side of the cliff, he knew where the man's hidden perch was, he would work towards it from above, it had took Wade more than an hour working around the face of the cliff, Wade could see Mary below, but she could see nothing of either men, she kept her head down below the rocks and only peered out between the crack of the two, she could feel her heart beating in her chest . . .

Wade had worked his way to within fifty feet of the man's hideout, he set and watched patiently for some time, he didn't want to expose himself, incase the ambusher had moved to a different spot . . . Wade had waited for more than an hour, watching for any sign of movement, listening to every sound, the slightest crack of branch, anything . . . Wade moved closer and found the man had moved back up over the top of the mountain and gotten on his horse and left, he stood up and whistled for Mary, she was greatly relieved to see Wade standing in open sight, he motioned for her to come on up . . .

When Mary climbed to the ambushers perch, Wade pointed down, the man wore flat soled boots, it was the same man, and there were a good dozen butts of rolled tobaccos, it seemed he had been here waiting for some time . . .

Wade traced their ambusher's tracks back to his horse, studying each and every step . . . When the man reached his horse, he stepped in some ground that was damp with moisture, leaving a perfect imprint of his right boot, Wade kneeling down, brushing away what little dirt had been knocked into the imprint, looking up at Mary and pointing down to the track, the heel of the man's right boot had the corner cut off the heel, about a quarter inch of it was missing and in the center of the heel imprint was a manufacturer label of a four leaf clover . . .

"We find the man wearing these boots and we find the man wanting us dead, I'd like to go after him, but we can't get the horses up this cliff here and he has at least a two hour jump on us right now . . . Let's go home Mary Tavner" . . .

"Wade, I would like nothing better right now than to see our home" . . .

"Mary, I fear the worst for our home, I am afraid when we get there, it will be no more than a ruble of ashes, burnt to the ground" . . .

"House or no house, it's still home to me Wade, we can rebuild the cabin" . . .

They make their way back down to the bottom of the canyon they were riding through and retrieve the horses . . . The horses being fresh from the rest and fresh grass and cool water, set out at a good pace, Wade giving the big palomino his head with slack reigns, the more ground he could cover the better, Mary and her black close beside abreast, it was good riding here . . .

It was nearing dusk as they climbed the last stretch of mountain which would drop them down into their valley, they had rode in from the west, a rougher stretch of riding, but it shortened it by several miles as from coming in from the north end of the valley, reigning up as Wade could smell the hint of wood smoke, fearing it was more than likely the remains of their cabin, Wade slides the Winchester from it's scabbard and holds it across the saddle, his right hand in the lever . . . They work their way around the last clump of rocks and trees that has them hidden from view of the cabin, Wade steps down from the saddle and Mary does likewise, peering around the last rock outcropping, Wade can see the cabin, it's still as they left it, but a thin line of smoke drifting from the stone flue, some one was in their cabin . . . Wade hands Mary the Winchester and pulls his Colt, leaving the horses tied, they quietly work their way down the slope . . . The horses are nervous as well, not wanting to stay behind, they know as well they are home . . . They wade across the creek and slip close to the corrals which have been put back in place, five horses inside, three of Wades and two others, an anger burns within Wade as they work closer to the house, the door creaks as it starts to open as the latch swings loose, Wade and Mary not standing more than twenty feet now from their porch, Wade has the Colt aimed at the front door as Mary has the Winchester leveled off too, Wades eyes searching around in other directions also, they are out in the open with no cover of any kind, the door swings open and standing in the doorway is Willy Stone, the tall lanky youngster that helped with the drive . . .

Willy is taken by shock nearly as he stands there with two guns pointed directly at him, but making out the faces in what dim light is left of the day: "Good Lord of Mercy, I thought you all were never coming back, man am I glad to see the two of you, rumor has it in town that you were both killed or something, ah heck, we knew better than that, Bob, come out here, look who's here" . . .

Bob Mocker steps out from the cabin as well, wearing new britches and a black leather vest fitting neatly around his chest and sporting a new holster with a new colt tied down low . . .

Wade smiles and gives them both a hardy handshake, Mary gives them both hugs . . . Wade looking them over: "Willy, you ain't changed a bit, but now Bob, you look like a new man here with all these new duds you got on, I see you traded that ole Schofield for a new sidearm, looks like you done went and spent your wages" . . .

"Yes sir, I sort of liked that colt you wear and thought I needed one too, it does handle nice don't it" . . .

Wade caught a glimpse of metal just under the left side of Bob's vest and reaches over and pushes the vest to the side just a bit, revealing a deputy's badge . . . "Well Bob, what on earth you wearing there"? as Wade smiles in approval . . .

"A lot of things have changed in the last couple of months in Silver Creek Springs, my pa, he's been elected the town sheriff, and well, I am serving as his deputy for now, I just rode out to check on Willy here, we got things put back in place out here, Ted and John helped us get all the cattle rounded back up and all, and well Willy here, he's been setting watch over your alls place, some strange things going on though around here, the cattle in the high meadow were spooked bad the other day, maybe it was just a wolf or bear, but they were nearly wild acting" . . .

About that time Wade and Mary were nearly knocked to the ground from behind as Roscoe had heard their voices and came running from the barn and jumped up on them both . . . He stood up on Mary and wrestled her to the ground as she was hugging on the big dog and roughing him up . . . "Oh big fellow, I thought you were dead" as Roscoe tries his best to lick her face . . .

Wade steps towards the cabin: "Well boys, I sure hope you got some fresh coffee a brewing" . . .

Willy jumps up on the porch just ahead of Wade: "Yes sir, we sure do, I just knew you were coming back, I just knew it"!

"Come on in boys, our home is as good as yours" . . .

Night had quickly fell into Three Valleys Ranch, the fire in the cabin felt good and the fresh coffee tasted even better, the fire putting on a constant heat that warmed the cabin and felt good to the bones . . . Wade and the two boys set at the table discussing the events that had took place, the two boys dying to hear every word of the story . . . Mary was working diligently fixing a pot of stew for them all, and after it was done she joined them at the table . . .

Their own bed felt good as they snuggled in for the night, the two boys were going to sleep in the barn, but Wade and Mary refused they sleep out there, as they fixed them blankets on the floor close to the fire . . . They had grown quite fond of all four of the boys . . .

Morning rolled around and Wade was up well before daylight, he planned to ride to town, there was business to take care of, serious business . . .

Wade was packing a small lunch to take along, as it was a good days ride, as Mary and Bob had also gotten up . . . Mary looking at the lunch he was packing in his saddlebags: "And just where are you planning on going Mr. Tavner" her eyes revealing a very serious look . . .

"Mary, I am going to town, things need to be resolved, and the sooner the better" . . .

Bob stepped up: "Do you know who is behind all of this"?

"Not for sure, I have an idea, I can't rightly prove it just now" . . .

Mary looking disgusted at him, "Don't go today, wait a few days Wade, we just got home" . . .

Bob puts his arm on Wades: "Wade, I am headed back to town this morning, tell me who you think might be behind all of this and I will talk to my Pa, he is the town sheriff now you know, let us handle this, it is our job" . . .

"Bob, my idea of who is responsible is just that, my idea, and I will keep it to myself, You go on back to town and talk with your Pa, but I will be in town in a few days" . . .

Bob and Wade walk out to the corral and Bob starts to saddle his gelding, Wade notices he has a loose shoe, "Bob, you can't ride him back to town like that, he will throw that shoe and might even end up lame, take my horse and I will put new shoes on yours and ride to town in a couple of days and we'll swap out" . . .

They agree and Bob throws his saddle on Wade's big gelding, "He's a lot of horse Bob, he'll spoil you from riding that little bay you got there" as Wade smiles at him . . .

Bob reins the big gelding around and heads out, "Maybe we won't trade back then", as he laughs as he heads out across the open valley . . .

Wade saddles a young bay gelding in the corral and leads him to the cabin, Mary and Willy were standing there on the porch, Mary's eyes had a gleam of pure happiness in them from being home and watching Wade walk across the yard . . .

"I'm going to ride up to the high meadows and check on the cattle up there, if they have it eat down good, it will be time to bring them back down into the lower valley, winter will be here before we know it, Willy, you got any plans"?

"Well no sir, I really don't" . . .

"Willy, I was thinking that I believe we could use a hand here full time, it won't pay too much, but we got that extra room on the back where Ramos stayed and we could feed you good" . . .

Willy jumped off that porch in a split second, sticking out his hand to Wade: "You got yourself a deal" with a smile that reached plum across his face . . .

"Well you help Mary around here today, I'm going up in the high meadows, keep your gun handy and eyes open" . . .

Wade stepped into the saddle and pulls the head of the young bay around and heads him down the valley and up the steep trail leading to the upper meadows . . . Riding along checking the grass and checking cattle as he goes, but he has more in mind . . . When he reaches the far end of the high country, he ties off his horse and climbs the steep slope to where he found the diggings before he left months ago . . . Searching around he finds it, there had been more diggings, and one man camped here for some time, and another man visiting from time to time, the tracks were fairly old and not any good plain markings . . . Wade slides back down the slope towards his horse, and rides slowly along the small stream that flowed in the upper valley, he finds another camp, and a hand built sluice box, Wade searched around the camp for some time, but again nothing fresh of signs, before he leaves, he takes a hefty rock and crushes the sluice box and destroys it and sends the remains floating down stream . . .

It was nearly noon as the sun was high over head, Wade had seen enough, but nothing either, nothing to tell him who was there, he rode back down into the lower valley, the breeze drifted in from the north, he swore he could smell Mary's cooking two miles downwind, as he lets the bay gelding pick up the pace towards the barn lot, a quarter mile out, Wade notices his big palomino back in the lot, Mary and Willy both standing there with a concerned look on their faces, as he gets closer, he sees blood on the big horses neck and shoulder . . .

"What happened, where's Bob"?

Mary's eyes slightly watered up, "We don't know, your horse just showed up a few minutes ago, Bob wasn't on him" . . .

Wade looked over the big horse, he had no wounds, the blood had to be Bob's . . . Wade stepped back into the saddle . . .

"Wade" . . .

"Mary, don't even think about stopping me, I'm going to find Bob, he has to be along the trail somewhere" . . .

"Wade, just be careful, please" . . .

"Mary, you and Willy don't be standing out in the open, keep your eyes peeled, I'll be back as soon as I find Bob" . . .

Wade pulled the bay around and took a fast pace out the end of the valley hitting the trail hard . . . but keeping an eye on Bob's tracks, he knew the tracks of his horse easily and Bob was just riding back to town . . . He hadn't rode more than an hour when he saw Bob lying beside the trail, partially propped up against a rock . . .

"I figured you'd be along as soon as your horse showed back up" . . . Bob was holding his neckerchief against his left shoulder . . .

"Are you hurt bad Bob, let me have a look here" . . . It was a clean wound he'd been shot just between his shoulder and his neck, just below his collar bone, just missing the bone, the bullet had gone clean through . . . Wade doctored him up the best he could . . .

"Your going to live alright, but you're going to be pretty darn sore for several days, let's get you back to the cabin, we can clean this up good and make sure no infection gets in there" . . .

"Wade I laid there pretending to be dead, halfway under cover, only leaving my legs sticking out and not moving, but I had my gun in my hand under me, there was probably a good hour passed before I heard a horse riding out, towards town" . . .

Riding back into the valley just before dark falls, Bob setting in the saddle weaving back and forth and Wade leading the bay gelding . . . Mary and Willy rush out to help, and take him inside and lay him down on some thick blankets close to the fire, where it is the warmest . . . Mary cleans the wound better, front and back, Wade walks over with a small bottle of a reddish orange colored liquid . . .

"You better bite down on something Bob, this iodine is going to burn like fire, there's no telling you it ain't going to hurt, but it will keep the infection out" . . .

Bob felt like he was going to pass out nearly, but kept the pain inside, fresh bandages were wrapped around the wound, he ate a small amount of soup and a cup of coffee and then fell asleep, Mary pulled the blankets up around him . . . It was a cloudy night and dark had encompassed the cabin and the entire valley . . .

They had all turned in for the night, but there was no sleep for Wade as he laid there pondering the situation, he knew that whoever shot Bob, thought he was shooting him since Bob was riding his horse, that bullet was intended for him, anger burned deep within his bones . . . There was at least two hours before daylight when Wade saddled his horse and led him out of the valley, so not to make any noise and awake anyone . . . Once out on the trail towards town he opened up the pace . . . Reaching the spot where Bob had been shot, Wade searched the area ahead of where Bob was laying, he found the tracks, a man setting in wait behind some rocks, a man who smoked rolled tobacco, a man wearing flat soled boots with the corner cut off the right heel and a slight impression of a four leaf clover . . . The assailant had gotten back on his horse and the tracks led back to town, whoever it was more than likely thought he had killed Wade . . .

Wade steps back into the saddle, heading towards town, but riding cautiously, stopping often, watching, looking, listening to every sound, looking at the tracks on the trail, only a couple sets of fresh tracks, those of Bob's horse heading out to the ranch the day before, and those of the man who had shot Bob . . . Wade rode with his Winchester in hand . . .

Mary awakes as the sun is peering through cracks in the doorway, putting on her clothes she steps into the living area, Bob is setting up, looking alert . . .

"Good morning Bob, glad to see you looking so good this morning, is Wade out checking cows already"?

"Ma'am, I've been awake for some time, and I haven't seen hide nor hair of Wade" . . .

Willy steps to the front door, "I see Wade done lit out on his horse early this morning, looked like he walked him out a ways before he got on him though for some reason" . . .

Mary's eyes snap: "Willy, saddle my horse, I know he's gone to town, there's going to be big trouble" . . .

Bob getting to his feet: "I'm going too, get me a horse saddled too" . . .

"Bob, you are in no shape to ride, not yet" . . .

"Sorry Mrs. Tavner, there ain't no stopping me from riding to town with you, me and Willy are both going" . . . The three of them head into town . . .

Wade Tavner rides into town mid afternoon, he followed the tracks all the way in, leading to the livery stable, he steps down from the saddle and leads his horse in . . . Jim Wilson was putting shoes on a gray mare . . .

"Good to see you Wade, want me to stall that horse for you" . . .

"Yeah, give him some oats too, he's put in a lot of miles lately, I hear Bill Mocker has been elected town sheriff, you know where I could find him this afternoon"?

"Well Wade, he's got an office at the other end of town, not much of an office, no jail cells or nothing, but you might find him there, you got a problem or troubles" . . .

"His boy's been shot, and I tracked the man who shot him right here to your livery, whoever it was probably rode in here late yesterday evening" . . .

"Well gosh Wade, that could have been nearly anyone in town" . . .

"I'll go talk with Bill, his boy will be ok" . . .

Wade walked quickly to the far end of town, the boardwalks creaked under each step, a sound he normally liked to hear, but now it seemed to make him nervous, as he knew there was a man in town who wanted him dead, reaching the new sheriff's office, he stepped in . . . Wade had never met Bill Mocker, but standing before him stood a man who had way too much resemblance to his son not to recognize who he was . . .

"Can I help you sir:?

Wade holding out his hand: "My name's Wade Tavner, we need to talk Bill" . . .

A smile draws across Bill's face: "My boy speaks mighty highly of you Mr. Tavner" . . .

"Well I think you got a right good boy there Bill" . . .

Bill's smile quickly turns to a look of concern: "Is there a problem with Bob"?

"He's been shot, he's going to be fine, sore for a few days for sure, he's out at my place right now, resting" . . .

"Who shot him and why"?

"I believe whoever shot him was trying to kill me, Bob was riding my horse back to town yesterday morning" . . .

"Do you know who did this"?

"Bill, what can you tell me about Wesley Simmons"?

"Well Wade, he's our banker here in town, he's loaned a lot of money to folks to get this here town off it's feet, he's a fine respectable man" . . .

Wade tells the sheriff of the tracks of the man's boots and the signs he has seen . . . "I got me some business down there at the bank, and I think I'll have a talk with Mr. Simmons while I am there" . . .

"I'll be along directly, we got some talking to do" . . .

Wade walks out of the sheriff's office and heads down the street to the bank, Wade always had an uneasy feeling for this Simmons fellow . . . He stepped up onto the boardwalk leading into the bank, cautiously removing the tie down strap from his colt, lifting it slightly making sure it was free and setting it back into the holster gently . . . Stepping into the bank he sees two other customers standing in front of the teller's window, the little teller man sees Wade enter and quickly turns to his boss, Mr. Simmons, Wade noticed him cringe slightly as he made eyesight. But Wade remembered the last time he saw the teller, that he had threatened to kill him, it was Mr. Simmons who he wished to talk with anyway . . . Walking closer to Mr. Simmons's desk, Wade noticed the ashtray with rolled tobaccos in it . . .

Wesley Simmons looked up just as Wade approached his desk, a flushed look took over his pale appearance as if Wade Tavner was the last man on earth he expected to see, his right arm nonchalantly slid under his desk as though he was scratching his leg or something . . .

Bill Mocker stepped into the bank just minutes behind Wade . . .

Wade leaned over on his desk, but before he spoke a word he heard the revolver cock, it was to late as the gun boomed underneath the desk, shooting up through the top of the wooden desk, splinters of wood shattering, twice it echoed into the small bank building, the two other customers quickly ran out into the street, Wade palmed his colt, but heard another shot that rang out behind him, Wade felt a stinging pain in his neck and another one in his chest, he felt the blood tricking down the side of his neck and across his shoulder from the wound in his neck, and more blood trickling down his chest, he turned and looked behind him where the third shot rang out, colt leveled off, and there stood Bill Mocker, who had fired and hit Mr. Simmons dead center, who now laid backwards in his chair, Wade felt himself swaying but quickly pointed his colt at the little teller . . .

"Don't shoot mister, it wasn't me, it was Wesley who wanted you gone, he wanted your ranch, he said there was gold on it, he wanted you killed in the worst way, he thought he killed you yesterday" . . .

Wade was about to fall to the floor, Bill Mocker caught him and helped him out the front door, Wade holstered his colt, setting on the doorstep of the bank . . . Bill hollered for some one to get help . . .

Mary and Bob and Willy had just rode into town, seeing the crowd that had gathered around the bank building quickly rode to it . . . Mary seeing Wade setting there, his shirt soaked in blood nearly went into panic . . . Both bullets had missed Wade, but a couple of two inch splinters of the oak desk top had lodged in Wade's neck and chest leaving a nasty wound that bled profusely . . .

Bill Mocker stood up, he's going to be ok, let's get him laid down and these wounds cleaned, as he sees his own son Bob, and walks over and hugs him . . .

Bob looks at Wade, "Glad your going to be ok, I just got one request" . . .

"And what would that be Bob"?

"I want to be the one who pours that iodine on those wounds" . . . as they both laugh . . .

Wade looks at Mary who is in total tears: "It's ok, I'll be fine, have the sheriff look at Simmons right boot" . . .

Mary walks over with Bill Mocker and he lifts Mr. Simmons right boot, flat soled boots revealing a cut off portion of the right heel and an imbedded imprint of a four leaf clover . . .

Bill looked at his son and then at Wade: "This is the man, all those signs you told me about, it was Mr. Simmons who tried to kill you" . . .

Wade stands back to his feet, putting his arm around Mary with help from Willy: "Lets go home" . . .

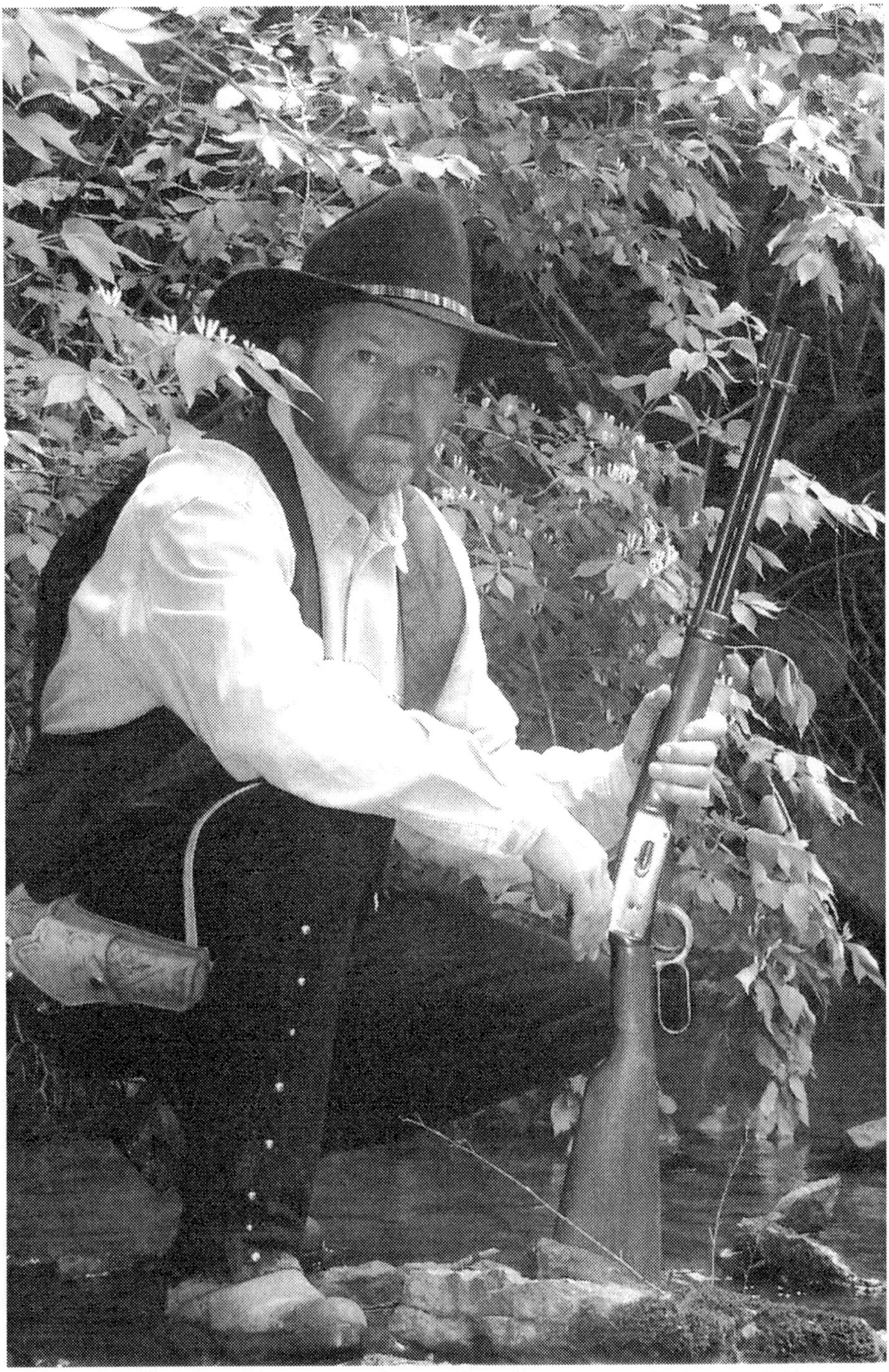

Chapter 17

Three Valleys Ranch continued to grow over the next several years, and became a cornerstone of the community . . . With Horned Herefords replacing the longhorns they had started with, with later generations of Tavners adding Black Angus bulls producing some of the finest black white-faced cattle in the territory . . .

Wade and Mary raised two sons, Joshua and Jeremiah, who eventually took over the ranch and more than doubled it in size, finding ways to irrigate the outer prairie land which made the grass grow green and lush in what used to be wasteland . . .

Willy Stone stayed on and became the ranch manager over the years and kept records of every calf born on the place and built the herd into strong bloodlines . . . Wade gave him ten acres at the far south end of the valley where he built a cabin to live, you very seldom saw Willy when he wasn't setting a top a horse . . . Willy married a gal named Laura, from Silver Creek Springs and never had any children of their own, but loved Wade's and Mary's just as much, Joshua and Jeremiah called them their Aunt and Uncle . . .

Bob Mocker became the US Territorial Marshal after serving several years as Silver Creek Springs Sheriff, stopping as often as he could just to set and visit with good friends . . . Willy had told Wade's two boys many times of how foolish Bob looked at trying to outdraw their pa on that first cattle drive, and it seemed that they never tired of hearing the past stories of their pa, and Willy was quite the story teller, Wade would smile as it seemed those stories seemed to get a tad bit bigger each time they were told . . .

Mary was the best of mother's to those two boys, learning them to read and write and the differences between right and wrong and also of proper and what was etiquette and not . . .

Wade taught them to ride and rope and shoot straight and how to spit and a few bad words just to make it a challenge for Mary, and that there was nothing more worthy than an honest man . . .

Silver Creek Springs had took a drastic change over the years, as the ore ran out, so did most of the population, but what few remained were good family folks, people who worked hard, honest folks, it had took a foot hold in the area, a beautifully landscaped area . . . The streams cleared up after all the mining operations folded up, trees grew back and covered the slopes of the mountains . . . The folks that stayed, raised cattle and horses and grew crops of wheat and barley, a few even raised tators . . . The Tavners helped numerous families get started with small herds of cattle at the fairest of prices . . .

Ted Hooper bought the general store and opened up a freighting exchange with financial help from Wade and Roger McNall, which turned into a thriving business in the area . . .

Roger McNall would visit during the summer and loved to catch cutthroat trout from the area streams . . .

John Black moved on to California with his dad in search of more gold fields . . .

Mary's Aunt Martha and Uncle Bill sold their general store back in Ft. Douglas, in their older years and moved to Three Valleys Ranch and lived out their lives there . . . Bill loved to set along side the stream and fish, Martha would set and watch him and quilt while listening to the relaxing sound of the river . . . They loved watching Joshua and Jeremiah grow up, as this was the same as their grandchildren . . . Mary would ride by and make a daily stop to see how they were getting along, and share a cup of coffee with them . . .

Wade Tavner passed away at the age of 87, Mary soon followed ten days later, not desiring to live any longer without her soul mate beside her, they are both laying in rest fifty feet from the west side of their cabin which still stands today, gravesites that grow the prettiest wild flowers of the valley each spring . . . The secret of the gold that lay hidden in the land of Three Valleys Ranch was buried with Wade . . .

A fourth generation of Tavners lives on the ranch today, which is still a prosperous and productive ranch . . .

Wade and Mary left a legacy behind, instilled in each generations heart, for the love of the land, just as God created it, and that wealth is not what you hold in your hand, but what you hold in your heart . . .